Love and Hate Story

Chris Mathes

Edited by Cypress Canyon Publishing
Brookings, South Dakota

ISBN: 978-1-7346082-8-1

Paperback Edition

Cover design by Cypress Canyon Publishing
Interior formatting by Cypress Canyon Publishing

Printed in the United States of America

Dedication

This book is dedicated to my parents. I thank them for who I am. Without them, I would not be where I am today.

Introduction

WHAT MAKES SOMEONE CHOOSE love instead of hate?

Or hate instead of love?

Every life is shaped by that choice—sometimes in ways we never expect.

Life is filled with questions like these—questions about who we are, why we act the way we do, and what purpose we serve in this world. No two people are exactly alike. Each of us carries our own story, shaped by our experiences, beliefs, and the choices we make along the way.

Because of that, the idea of "normal" becomes difficult to define. What is normal, really? Is there a correct way for someone to think, behave, or live their life? At some point, most of us wonder where we fit into the world and whether the way we see things is the way they are meant to be seen.

Life itself is influenced by many forces, but two stand above the rest—two powerful emotions that shape how we see others and how we respond to the world around us: **love and hate**.

Love is something we believe exists everywhere, or at least we hope it does. Yet love is not a simple idea. It is a powerful word that carries many meanings. For some, love is kindness. For others, it is sacrifice, loyalty, or forgiveness. What does love look like to you? What does it feel like? The answer is never exactly the same from one person to another.

But where love exists, hate often follows close behind. Hate can grow from misunderstanding, pain, fear, or anger. It can divide people, shape opinions, and influence how we respond to the world and to one another.

The truth is, we do not live in a world of constant love, happiness, and perfection. But imagine if we did. What would that world look like? Would it truly be perfect, or would something essential be missing?

Our world is made up of countless people, cultures, and perspectives. Different backgrounds. Different stories. Different ways of understanding life. This diversity is what gives the world its richness. It is like a massive painting made up of millions of brushstrokes, each person adding their own color to the larger picture.

Because of this, life can be seen in many ways. Yet time and again, two powerful forces continue to shape the direction of our lives: love and hate.

Did you think life was always rainbows and roses? Of course not. Still, many of us wish it could be. That hope is part of what drives us forward. It reminds us not to take life—or the people in it—for granted.

The story you are about to read lives in the complicated space between love and hate. It explores how easily one can lead to the other, and how the choices we make can shape the course of a life in ways we never expected.

If words hold so much power, why do we sometimes choose words filled with hatred instead of kindness? Perhaps the answer lies in the complexity of human nature. A world where everything felt the same might be peaceful, but it would hardly be interesting. Variety gives life depth—but it also comes with consequences.

In the pages ahead, you will step into a story that many people might think they understand. But how well do we ever truly know another person? Behind every life are motivations, struggles, and emotions that remain hidden beneath the surface.

Sometimes the line between love and hate is thinner than we realize. And sometimes a single moment—a single choice—can change everything.

This story reveals those hidden layers. It is a story shaped by love, challenged by hate, and guided by the complicated decisions that fall somewhere in between.

And by the end, you may find yourself asking the same question with which we began:

What truly makes someone choose love instead of hate?

So sit back, and prepare yourself for a journey through the twists, turns, and emotional highs and lows of a life that may not be as simple as it first appears.

Chapter 1:
Home for the Summer

SUMMER HAD ARRIVED IN SUNNY FLORIDA, and Miami was already alive with energy.

The beaches were crowded with families enjoying the bright morning sun. Children ran through the sand building castles near the water while others splashed in the warm waves. Surfers drifted across the rolling tide, waiting patiently for the next perfect swell.

Music floated across the beach from portable speakers. Volleyball games kicked up clouds of sand while friends laughed and called out to each other. Coolers were opened, drinks were passed around, and families gathered under umbrellas for picnics.

For many people, summer in Miami meant sunshine, freedom, and memories waiting to be made.

But summer also had another side.

It was a season where emotions ran high—where relationships began, ended, or sometimes exploded entirely. Love and hate often lived closer together than anyone wanted to admit.

And for one eighteen-year-old, this summer was about to change everything.

Ryan Mulligan woke to the distant rumble of traffic drifting through his bedroom window. He groaned and rolled onto his back, squinting at the sunlight spilling across the ceiling.

9:03 a.m.

Friday.

The first full week of summer break.

Normally, that would have felt like freedom. Instead, Ryan lay there staring at the clock for a few seconds longer than necessary.

Julie.

The thought slipped into his mind before he could stop it. He sighed and sat up.

Outside, Miami was already buzzing with life. Cars rushed down the street, dogs barked somewhere nearby, and the warm Florida sun promised another hot day.

Ryan stretched and ran a hand through his hair.

Perfect beach weather.

He dragged himself out of bed and shuffled into the bathroom, splashing cold water on his face. A few minutes later, he stepped into the shower, letting the hot water run over his shoulders while he tried to shake the thoughts lingering in his head.

It hadn't worked.

Julie still crept into his mind whether he liked it or not.

After getting dressed, Ryan headed downstairs following the delicious aroma of the promise of breakfast coming from the kitchen. Eggs sizzled on the stove while bacon crackled in a pan. Toast popped up from the toaster.

His father sat at the table reading something on his iPad while Ryan's younger sister, Kate, quietly ate a bowl of cereal. Their mother stood at the stove cooking.

Ryan grabbed a glass and poured himself some orange juice before dropping into a chair. He leaned back, still half asleep.

"Good morning," his mom said with a small smile. "Didn't expect you up this early."

She placed a plate in front of him. Scrambled eggs, bacon, and toast.

"Morning," Ryan replied groggily. "Guess I couldn't sleep anymore."

His dad glanced up from the iPad. "Got any plans today?"

Ryan shrugged. "Probably meeting up with Jim. Maybe hit the beach."

"That sounds like a pretty good day," his dad said.

His mom turned toward him. "Just be careful."

Ryan sighed. "I will."

"You know how things get down there," she added.

Ryan raised an eyebrow. "Mom, I'm eighteen."

"That doesn't mean I stop worrying."

Ryan smiled slightly. "I'll be fine."

After finishing breakfast, he gave his sister a quick kiss on the forehead and grabbed his keys. "See you guys later."

"Have fun," his mom called.

Outside, the Florida heat wrapped around him immediately. The neighborhood was alive with activity—people walking dogs, mowing lawns, loading coolers into cars.

Summer had officially begun.

Ryan climbed into his car and backed out of the driveway. A few minutes later he pulled up outside his friend Jim's house. Jim answered the door with a grin.

"About time."

Ryan laughed. "You ready?"

"Always."

Jim grabbed his sunglasses and jumped into the passenger seat.

"So," Ryan said as they drove off, "what's the plan?"

"Beach," Jim said immediately.

Ryan shook his head. "Of course."

Jim smirked. "Maybe smoke a little. Chill out."

Ryan rolled his eyes. "Man, that's literally all you think about."

Jim laughed. "Hey, it works."

Then he added casually, "Oh—and Julie's throwing a party tonight."

Ryan's grip tightened slightly on the steering wheel.

"Didn't know that."

"Parents are out of town."

Ryan stared at the road.

"You should come," Jim said.

Ryan exhaled slowly.

"Not sure that's a great idea."

"Come on, man. Maybe talk to her."

Ryan shook his head. "She's the one who ended things."

"Maybe she regrets it."

Ryan didn't answer. A few minutes later they reached the beach.

The shoreline was packed with people enjoying the day. Waves rolled gently toward the sand while music and laughter filled the air.

Ryan stepped out of the car and scanned the crowd. Off to the side, Ryan could see Julie in the near distance with a couple of her girlfriends in the water. He figured she would be there. Julie had always loved the beach, especially during the summer.

Ryan paused for a moment, watching her from where he stood.

Ryan remembered holding Julie on this same beach a year earlier, both of them laughing under the same moonlight. At the time he thought it was perfect. But standing there now, he couldn't shake the strange feeling that something about those memories had always felt slightly… incomplete.

He pushed the thought aside and walked toward her.

Julie looked up and noticed him. Ryan lifted a hand in a small wave, and she smiled.

"Hey, Julie."

"Hey, Ryan," she said. "How are you?"

"Good," he replied. "You?"

She nodded as a reply. "I heard you might come tonight."

Ryan smirked. "Jim spreading the word already?"

Julie laughed. "You should come. No expectations. Just a party."

Ryan thought about it for a moment. "All right," he said.

"Come around nine," she said.

Ryan nodded. "See you then," he said before he walked back toward his friends, unsure what the night might bring.

The afternoon passed quickly—music, drinks, tacos from a food truck, and the slow drift of time under the hot Florida sun. By the time the sky began to darken and the first stars appeared, Ryan leaned back in the passenger seat while Jim drove them home.

Julie's party.

Nine o'clock.

Ryan stared out the window at the glowing Miami skyline. Something about tonight felt different.

He couldn't explain why. But deep down, he had the strange feeling that this summer—this night— was about to change everything.

Chapter 2
The Party

THE NIGHT AIR WAS WARM and heavy with humidity, though a soft breeze drifted in from the ocean and softened the lingering heat of the day. A bright full moon hung over Miami, casting pale light across the streets and beaches. Full moons had a reputation for bringing chaos—or maybe they simply revealed what people were already capable of.

The city pulsed with nightlife. Music drifted from bars and beach houses, headlights swept across crowded streets, and laughter echoed through the humid air. It was the kind of night where anything could happen.

Ryan and Jim pulled up outside Julie's house just after nine. Cars lined both sides of the street, and people spilled across the front lawn and driveway. Music blasted from the backyard, the bass vibrating through the walls of the house and into the night.

"Looks like half of Miami showed up," Ryan muttered as he stepped out of the car.

Jim grinned and stretched his arms. "Julie always throws a good party. You should know that by now."

They followed the steady stream of people through the house and into the backyard. The pool area was packed with bodies moving to the music. Some people danced near the speakers while others lounged around the water with drinks in their hands, their laughter blending into the thumping bass.

Ryan scanned the crowd near the pool. Girls in bikinis laughed and danced in the flashing lights, but his attention drifted elsewhere without him realizing it. A group nearby shouted loudly over a game of beer pong, and several people splashed around in the pool while tossing a volleyball back and forth in a loose attempt at a game. The air smelled strongly of chlorine, alcohol, and weed. Ryan paused for a moment, taking in the chaos around him before leaning closer to Jim, so he could be heard over the music.

"I'm gonna grab us some drinks," Ryan said.

Jim nodded and pointed toward a table near the pool. "Cool. I'll be over there."

Ryan pushed through the crowd toward the makeshift bar someone had set up along the patio. He grabbed two Bud Lights from a cooler, popped them open, and started walking back toward the table. As he moved through the crowd, he scanned the faces around him, recognizing a few classmates and neighbors mixed among strangers he had never seen before.

Near the back fence, partly hidden in shadow, Ryan noticed someone standing alone. The guy appeared to be about Ryan's age, maybe a little older, and he wasn't talking to anyone. Instead, he seemed to be watching the crowd with an unusual focus.

For a brief moment, Ryan had the strange feeling the guy wasn't watching the party.

He was watching him.

Ryan frowned slightly and slowed his step. When he looked again a moment later, the guy had vanished into the shifting crowd of people. Ryan shook the feeling off and continued toward the table, deciding it was probably nothing.

Jim took the beer immediately when Ryan handed it to him. Julie and her friend, Katie, looked up as Ryan sat down across from them.

"Hey, Ryan," Julie said with a small smile. "How's it going?"

"I'm good," Ryan replied, glancing around at the crowded yard. "This party got huge. Where did all these people come from?"

Julie laughed softly and took a sip of her beer. "Friends of friends. Word spreads fast."

Ryan raised an eyebrow and leaned back in his chair. "I'm a little surprised you invited me tonight… after everything."

Julie hesitated before answering, her expression softening slightly. "I meant what I said earlier. The past is the past. We can still be friends."

Ryan nodded slowly, though he wasn't entirely sure how he felt about that. "Well… you definitely know how to throw a party."

She smiled. "Always have."

After a while Ryan wandered through the crowd, talking to people he recognized from school. The music, shouting, and flashing lights began to feel overwhelming after a few drinks, and the noise pressed against his head like static. Eventually he grabbed a quick shot of tequila and slipped away from the backyard without saying anything.

The beach was only a short walk from Julie's house. As Ryan stepped onto the sand, the pounding music faded behind him and the sound of waves rolling onto shore replaced it. The moon reflected across the water, and the ocean breeze cooled his skin as he stared out across the dark horizon.

For a moment everything felt calm.

Footsteps approached behind him, crunching softly in the sand. Ryan turned and saw Julie walking toward him, her arms wrapped loosely around herself against the breeze.

"I figured you'd be out here," she said quietly. "You always came out here when things got loud."

Ryan gave a small smile and looked back toward the water. "You know me."

"I do," she replied.

They stood side by side looking out at the ocean, both remembering nights that now felt very far away. They had spent countless evenings on this same beach walking along the shoreline, talking about their future and holding each other beneath the same moon now hanging over the water.

"That feels like forever ago," Ryan said after a moment.

Julie nodded slowly. "It does."

Silence stretched between them for several seconds before Julie spoke again. "I'm glad you came tonight," she said gently.

Ryan glanced down at the sand near his feet. "I didn't think I would."

"I wanted to see you," she said. "Even if things can't go back to the way they were."

Ryan felt a knot tighten in his chest but didn't respond. Julie wiped quickly at the corner of her eye before a tear could fall.

"I'm sorry for hurting you," she said. "But I knew it was over."

Before Ryan could say anything, someone shouted from the house.

"Hey! You two coming back in or what?"

Ryan turned toward the voice and raised his hand. "We'll be there in a minute!"

The voice laughed. "Hurry the hell up!"

Julie looked back toward the house and took a slow breath. "I should get back to the party," she said quietly.

She hesitated for a moment before adding, "It really was good to see you, Ryan."

"You too," he replied.

Julie turned and walked back toward the house, leaving Ryan standing alone with the sound of the ocean. After a minute he followed the path toward the yard, but instead of returning to the party he continued along the side walkway toward the front of the house.

Something about the night no longer felt right.

As he reached his car, someone called out behind him.

"Hey! Where the hell are you going?"

Ryan turned and saw Jim jogging toward him with a confused look on his face. "Dude, you're leaving already?"

Ryan shrugged and opened the car door. "Yeah. I think I need to."

"Come on, man," Jim said. "The party's just getting started."

"I know," Ryan replied, climbing into the driver's seat. "I just... can't tonight."

Jim watched him for a moment before finally shrugging. "All right. Your loss."

Ryan started the engine and pulled away from the curb, leaving the noise of the party behind him. Jim watched the taillights disappear down the street before turning and heading back toward the house, where the music continued pounding and the party grew wilder by the minute.

Ryan woke to the sound of his phone ringing beside his bed. He rolled over and squinted at the screen, recognizing Jim's name flashing across it. Instead of answering, he dropped the phone back onto the nightstand and stared up at the ceiling.

The clock beside the bed read **11:00 a.m.**

Ryan replayed the night in his mind while Julie's words echoed back to him.

I knew it was over.

Something about that didn't sit right.

Ryan rubbed his face, trying to piece together what had gone wrong between them. Julie had always said she wanted to see other people—that had been the explanation when things ended. But now it felt incomplete, like part of the story had been left out.

He sat up slowly as a thought formed in his mind that he had never fully allowed himself to consider. Maybe he hadn't loved Julie the way she loved him.

The realization sat heavily in his chest. If that was true, then maybe he had broken her heart long before she ended things.

An hour later, Ryan got dressed, grabbed something quick to eat downstairs, and headed out. He needed air, space, anything to clear his head. He drove around the city for a while with the windows down and music blasting while Miami buzzed with life around him.

Eventually, he parked near downtown and started walking. The late afternoon sun was beginning to sink toward the horizon, painting the sky orange and gold while people filled the sidewalks heading toward bars and clubs. Ryan moved quietly through the crowd, not really in the mood for any of it.

As he passed a row of clubs, he noticed a guy standing near one of the entrances handing out flyers. The guy looked about Ryan's age and seemed completely focused on the passing crowd.

Ryan walked past him.

Then he stopped.

He was sure he had heard something.

Ryan turned around and looked at the guy. "Did you say something to me?"

The guy looked confused and shook his head. "No."

Ryan frowned slightly. "All right… my mistake."

He turned to walk away, but a moment later he heard the voice again. Ryan spun around and walked back toward him.

"Okay, I definitely heard you say something."

The stranger tilted his head and studied him for a moment before speaking.

"You're not like the other people walking these streets tonight," he said calmly.

Ryan crossed his arms and looked at him carefully. "And how would you know that?"

The stranger didn't answer right away. Instead, he watched Ryan with a strange intensity that made Ryan uncomfortable.

Finally he spoke.

"You didn't come to the city tonight to drink," the stranger said quietly. "You came because something inside you feels wrong… and you don't know what it is."

Ryan felt a chill creep across the back of his neck.

"What are you talking about?"

The stranger stepped slightly closer and lowered his voice. "I can show you a world far bigger than the one you think you know," he said. "A world where you finally understand who you really are."

Ryan stared at him, unsure whether to laugh or walk away.

"What the hell does that mean?"

The stranger's smile widened slightly. "It means you're standing at the beginning of something," he said softly.

Then he leaned closer and whispered, "Let me show you who you really are."

Chapter 3
The Secret of the Night

THE SKY ABOVE MIAMI HAD TURNED DEEP BLACK, scattered with faint stars that flickered between drifting clouds. The nightlife of the city continued around them—music spilling from nearby clubs, distant traffic rolling through intersections, voices drifting down the sidewalks. Yet here on the concrete steps near the street corner, the world felt strangely still.

Ryan sat beside the stranger, trying to process everything the man had said. Only minutes earlier they had been complete strangers passing each other on the sidewalk. Now they were sitting together while Ryan struggled to understand why this guy seemed to know so much about him.

Finally Ryan leaned back against the step and turned toward him.

"So… what exactly is it you think you know about me?" Ryan asked. "Because right now, I'm dying to hear it."

The stranger chuckled quietly and glanced sideways at him. "You sure you're ready to hear it?"

Ryan shook his head in disbelief. "Man, I just met you. There's no way you know anything about me."

The stranger studied him carefully before answering. "Let's just say I notice things about people. Sometimes it's obvious. Sometimes it takes longer. But when you've seen it enough times, you start recognizing it."

Ryan smirked slightly. "What is that supposed to be, some kind of superpower?"

The stranger's smile faded.

"No," he said quietly. "It's not a superpower. If anything, it's more like something I didn't ask for but have to live with."

He lowered his head and stared at the pavement for a moment, and Ryan noticed the shift immediately. The confidence in the stranger's voice softened into something more personal.

"I didn't always understand it either," the man continued. "For a long time I thought something was wrong with me. Like I was different from everyone else in a way I couldn't explain. You spend years trying to act the way people expect, convincing yourself everything is normal."

He lifted his gaze toward the glow of the streetlights.

"But deep down you know something doesn't fit."

Ryan shifted slightly on the step. The words sounded uncomfortably familiar.

"One day you realize you can't keep pretending," the stranger continued. "You start asking yourself questions you've been avoiding your entire life. Questions about who you really are… and who you're supposed to be."

Ryan watched people pass along the sidewalk—groups of friends laughing, couples heading toward the clubs, taxis creeping slowly down the street. Everyone else seemed completely carefree.

Meanwhile Ryan felt like something inside him had started shifting.

"You ever feel like that?" the stranger asked.

Ryan hesitated before answering. "Maybe," he said quietly. "I don't know."

The stranger nodded as if he had expected that response.

"It's not easy figuring yourself out," he said. "Especially when the world isn't always kind to people who live differently."

Ryan rubbed his hands together and looked back toward the street. "I'm still not sure what you're getting at."

The stranger leaned forward, resting his elbows on his knees.

"Think about the way you've been feeling lately," he said. "Think about last night. You didn't leave that party because you were bored. You left because something about it felt wrong."

Ryan frowned slightly but didn't respond.

"You didn't come to the city tonight to drink," the stranger continued quietly. "You came because something inside you feels wrong… and you don't know what it is."

Ryan felt the words hit him harder than he expected.

"How could you possibly know that?" he asked.

The stranger shrugged slightly.

"Because I've been there."

For a moment neither of them spoke. The sounds of the city continued around them, but the space between them felt strangely quiet.

After several seconds Ryan spoke again.

"All right," he said. "Let's say you're right. Let's say something feels off. What exactly do you think it is?"

The stranger didn't answer immediately. Instead, he studied Ryan carefully, as if deciding whether he was ready to hear the truth.

"You've known for a long time," he finally said.

Ryan's stomach tightened.

"No I haven't."

"Yes," the stranger replied calmly. "You just didn't want to admit it."

Ryan looked away toward the street as memories began flashing through his mind—moments he had never fully examined, feelings he had pushed aside, thoughts he had buried the moment they surfaced.

"Take a minute," the stranger said gently. "You already know the answer."

Ryan sat there in silence while the realization slowly surfaced in his mind. It was something he had felt for years but never spoken aloud, something he had pushed away every time it appeared.

Ryan swallowed hard. "Just say it," he said finally.

The stranger met his eyes.

"You're gay."

The words settled between them, heavy and unavoidable.

Ryan felt as if the entire world had suddenly gone quiet. Deep down he knew the stranger was right. He had known for years, even if he had never allowed himself to say it.

But hearing someone else say it out loud made it real.

Ryan ran his hands through his hair and stared down at the sidewalk.

"My whole life," he murmured, "I kept telling myself it was nothing."

"That's how it starts for most of us," the stranger said softly.

Ryan leaned back against the step, feeling emotionally drained. His thoughts raced through years of memories that suddenly looked different from this new perspective.

"So what now?" Ryan asked quietly.

The stranger gave a small smile.

"Now you figure out what you want to do with the truth."

Ryan sat there thinking about everything that had just happened. His entire life suddenly looked different from the perspective he had always forced himself to ignore. Part of him felt terrified.

But another part of him felt something else.

Relief.

For the first time in years, the question he had avoided finally had an answer. And it was if a heavy weight had been lifted from his soul.

Ryan looked over at the stranger again. "How did you know?" he asked.

The man shrugged. "Like I said… sometimes you just recognize it."

He stood up and brushed the dust from his jeans before stepping back toward the corner where he had been handing out flyers earlier.

Ryan remained seated on the steps, staring out at the street while his thoughts spun in circles. Across the road people laughed and disappeared into the glow of the clubs, completely unaware that his entire world had just shifted.

For the first time in his life, Ryan wasn't sure who he was supposed to be anymore.

And he had no idea who would still be standing beside him when the truth finally came out.

Chapter 4
Realizing the Truth

THE NIGHT SLOWLY GAVE WAY TO MORNING as the sky shifted from deep black to a soft orange glow. The first light of day stretched across the horizon, pushing the darkness aside. What had felt like only a few minutes had somehow turned into hours.

Ryan had spent most of the night sitting on those steps, talking to a stranger who had somehow changed everything. He hadn't slept, only dozing off briefly, his thoughts too loud to let him rest.

Now the city was waking up. Cars filled the streets, people hurried along sidewalks, and the quiet stillness of the night was replaced with the steady rhythm of morning life. Ryan glanced around, realizing suddenly that the stranger was gone. He couldn't remember when he had left.

One moment he had been there. The next, he wasn't.

Ryan sat there a while longer, staring up at the brightening sky. A few clouds drifted overhead, and the sun rose steadily, promising another hot Miami day. Everything looked normal—almost too normal—considering how much had changed in the last twenty-four hours.

Because something *had* changed.

He could feel it.

This wasn't some passing thought he could push aside later. It was real now, and that meant he had to figure out what came next. Part of him wanted to find that guy again and ask a hundred more questions. The other part of him knew that wasn't exactly easy in a city this big.

Still, it was a start.

Ryan finally stood, brushed himself off, and started walking toward where he had parked his car. He was so deep in thought that when someone called his name, he stopped dead in his tracks.

"Ryan?"

He turned and saw a woman a short distance away, looking at him with puzzled surprise. It took him a second to process it.

It was his mom.

Ryan forced a smile, though his mind immediately started racing for an explanation.

"Ryan, what are you doing out here so early?" she asked. "We thought you stayed with friends last night."

"Hey, Mom," he said, trying to sound casual. "What are you doing out this morning?"

She didn't seem suspicious, only curious. "Running errands. Your dad wants to grill tonight, so I'm picking up a few things. I wasn't sure if you'd be home for dinner. Where were you?"

Ryan hesitated. He wasn't ready to tell her the truth—not even close. The words sat in his chest, but they weren't coming out. Not yet.

"I was just out with some friends," he said finally. "Ran into a bunch of people and ended up staying out pretty late. Then I came into the city for a bit. Thought I'd grab coffee before heading home."

She nodded, accepting it without question. "Well, I'm glad you had a good time. Just give us a heads-up next time, okay? We worry."

"I will," Ryan replied. "I'll be home later. In time for dinner."

She smiled warmly. "Good. I'll see you tonight."

"Love you, Mom."

"I love you too."

Ryan watched her walk away before letting out a slow breath. That had been close—too close. He wasn't ready to have that conversation, and he didn't even know how he would begin when the time came.

Not yet.

As he continued down the street toward his car, he noticed someone leaning against it. A young guy wearing dark sunglasses stood beside the driver's side door, casually smoking a cigarette. A black

Mustang GT was parked nearby, but this guy was clearly waiting by *Ryan's* car.

Ryan slowed.

No way.

The guy flicked the cigarette to the ground and crushed it under his foot before looking up.

"Well, well," he said with a grin. "Look who finally showed up."

Ryan stopped a few feet away. "What the hell are you doing here?"

"I figured you'd come back for your car eventually," the guy said. "Thought I'd wait around."

Ryan shook his head. "I thought you disappeared. I woke up and you were gone."

"Yeah," the guy replied casually. "I had stuff to do. But I wanted to check on you."

Ryan crossed his arms. "Why?"

The guy smiled slightly. "Because I told you—I can help you. We could grab some coffee, take a drive, talk a little more. I think you've got a lot of questions."

Ryan hesitated.

He did have questions.

"…Yeah," he said. "I do."

"Then let's go."

They got into Ryan's car and pulled out onto the street. The city was already alive around them, traffic moving steadily as the morning continued to unfold.

"So where are we going?" Ryan asked.

"I'll tell you where to go," the guy said. "Just drive."

Ryan nodded, then glanced over at him. "All right. Then let me ask you something. First, I don't even know your name."

"Nick," he said. "And you're Ryan, right?"

"Yeah," Ryan replied. "What's it like for you… living like this? Being out and just being yourself?"

Nick leaned back in his seat, thinking. "It's different for everyone. But once you stop fighting it, it feels easier. Not easy—but easier. You're not constantly pretending anymore."

Ryan kept his eyes on the road.

"I spent years trying to convince myself I was someone else," Nick continued. "Trying to fit into what people expected. But you can't keep lying to yourself forever. Eventually it catches up to you."

Ryan nodded slowly. "That's the part that scares me," he admitted. "Everything changes."

"Yeah," Nick said. "It does. But not all of it's bad."

Ryan let that sit for a moment. "I'm not ready to tell anyone. Not my family. Not my friends. I just need time."

"That's normal," Nick replied. "You'll know when you're ready. It has to be on your time—not anyone else's."

Ryan exhaled slowly, gripping the steering wheel a little tighter. "Yeah. I just don't want it getting out before I'm ready."

"It won't," Nick assured him. "As long as you take things at your own pace."

Ryan looked out the window briefly, watching the city pass by. For the first time, everything felt slightly different, like he was seeing the world through a new lens—uncertain, but also strangely freeing.

After a while, Ryan dropped Nick off and headed home. He pulled into the driveway just as the smell of burgers hit the air. His dad was already outside grilling, and his mom was setting things up on the patio.

For a moment, everything felt normal again.

But Ryan knew better.

After dinner, he went upstairs and collapsed onto his bed, exhaustion finally catching up to him. Within minutes, he was asleep.

Later that night, across the city, Nick walked slowly toward his house, his shoulders tense with every step. The neighborhood was run-down, the houses worn and neglected, the air heavy with silence. Even the porch lights on the street seemed dimmer there, as if the whole block had given up trying to look alive.

This wasn't a place that felt like home.

As he approached the front door, he hesitated, hoping maybe—just maybe—the house would be quiet. He opened it slowly and slipped inside, trying not to make a sound. The smell hit him first: booze, stale smoke, and the sour rot of a place where no one cared enough to keep anything clean.

He made it only partway toward the stairs before his father's voice tore through the house.

"Booooy!"

Nick froze.

"Where the fuck have you been?" his dad shouted from the other room. "Your mother's been worried sick. Don't stand there acting stupid. I asked you a question."

Nick clenched his jaw and turned around. "I was at a friend's house."

His father stepped into view, already drunk, already angry, his face red and slick with sweat. "You think I'm stupid?" he snapped. "You think I don't know when you're lying to me?"

Nick didn't answer.

That only made it worse.

His father moved closer, glaring at him with that same disgust Nick had seen a thousand times before. "I ought to beat your ass right now," he said. "You think you can come and go whenever the fuck you want?"

Nick's chest tightened. He didn't wait to hear more. He backed down the hallway, reached his bedroom, slipped inside, and slammed the door shut. He locked it just as the pounding started.

"Open this damn door!" his father roared. "You think you can hide from me?"

Nick backed away, his heart hammering as the whole frame shook under the force of the blows.

"I swear to God, boy, I'll break this fucking door down! You hear me? I'll lock you in this house and you'll never leave again. I'll beat your ass so red you won't sit right for a week."

Nick slid down against the door, breathing hard, tears burning in his eyes. He hated this. Hated how scared he still got. Hated how normal it had become. His whole body shook with fear and anger crashing together inside him.

This wasn't new.

But it never got easier.

Eventually the pounding stopped. The house fell quiet again, but Nick didn't trust it. He sat there listening to his own breathing, waiting for the next explosion.

Then something inside him shifted.

He stood up, wiped at his face, and crossed to his desk. From a box hidden in the back of the drawer, he pulled the money he had saved—about four hundred dollars, all of it scraped together from odd jobs, handing out flyers, doing whatever he could to stay out of the house and keep something for himself.

It wasn't much.

But it was enough to run.

He shoved the cash into his pocket and moved to the window.

Then he stopped.

Voices.

Yelling.

Coming from downstairs.

Nick crept to his bedroom door, cracked it just enough to hear, and the sound hit him like a slap. His father was screaming again, but this time it wasn't aimed at him.

It was his mother.

Nick's stomach dropped. He rushed out of the room and toward the kitchen.

The scene looked like a disaster zone. Broken plates littered the floor. Glass glittered across the tile. Pots and pans were scattered everywhere, and in the middle of it all stood his father, gripping a pan in one hand and towering over Nick's mother. A bruise was already blooming across her cheek, and tears streaked down her face as she whispered apologies for something that clearly wasn't her fault.

Something in Nick snapped.

He didn't think.

He grabbed the nearest pot and swung with everything he had. The metal connected with a hard crack, and his father dropped to the floor instantly, his body hitting the tile with a heavy thud.

Silence.

For half a second.

Then movement.

Nick rushed to his mother and helped her to her feet. His hands were shaking so badly he could barely hold onto her, but he managed to get her moving. "Come on," he said. "Come on, Mom. Come on."

They didn't stop until they were back inside his room with the door slammed shut behind them.

From downstairs came a groan.

Then footsteps.

Then rage.

"Boy! Where the fuck are you?" his father bellowed. "You don't want to fuck with me. I'll beat your ass into the ground! You hear me? You stay out of my goddamn business!"

Nick shoved his dresser against the door just as the pounding started again. The frame rattled, wood grinding against wood, while his father kicked and slammed against it from the other side.

Nick grabbed an ice pack from the small freezer in his room and pressed it gently to his mother's cheek. She winced, but held it there, trembling.

"Mom," he said, his voice breaking, "are you okay?"

She nodded weakly. "I'll be all right."

"No," Nick said, shaking his head. "No, this isn't all right. You can't stay here. Come with me. Please. I've got somewhere we can go."

Her eyes filled with tears. "I can't."

"Mom—"

"He'll find us," she whispered, gripping his hands. "You don't understand. He'll find us."

"I don't care," Nick said. "I'm not leaving you here with him."

"You have to."

The words hit harder than anything else.

The pounding on the door grew louder. His father's voice came through it in bursts of rage.

"Open this fucking door! You lying bitch, you open this goddamn door right now! I'll hunt both of you down if you leave me."

Nick flinched. His mother pulled him closer and looked him right in the eyes.

"Listen to me," she said, stronger now. "You go. You get out of here. You build a life. That's what matters now."

"I'll come back," Nick said, sobbing openly now. "I swear I'll come back for you."

"I know you will," she said softly. "But not today."

Another violent crash shook the door.

"Now go," she said. "Please."

Nick hesitated only a second longer. Then he moved as fast as he could, throwing clothes and whatever else he could grab into a bag. His hands shook so badly he nearly dropped everything.

At the window, he stopped and turned back.

"I love you," he said.

"I love you too," she answered, her voice breaking. "Now go."

Nick climbed out and dropped to the ground below. He looked up once and saw her at the window, watching him, one hand lifted weakly in goodbye. Then she shut it.

He ran.

The next morning the beach was quiet in the early morning light. Waves rolled gently onto the shore as the sun rose over the horizon, casting gold across the water.

Nick sat alone in the sand, staring out at the ocean. For the first time in a long time, he felt still.

Not safe.

But free.

A little.

Footsteps approached behind him. Nick tensed slightly before feeling a light tap on his shoulder. He turned and saw Ryan standing there.

"Hey," Ryan said. "What are you doing out here?"

Nick blinked in surprise, then gave a small, tired smile. "Just needed to get away."

Ryan nodded, understanding more than he said. "You got somewhere to go?"

Nick hesitated. "…Not really."

Ryan shifted slightly, then made a decision.

"You can stay with me for a while," he said. "If you need somewhere."

Nick looked at him for a long moment, as if weighing whether to trust him.

"Yeah," he said quietly. "I think I do."

Ryan nodded once. "All right. I'll come back for you later."

Ryan turned and started jogging again, but he already knew one thing for certain: by the end of the day, he wouldn't just be carrying his own secret anymore.

He'd be helping Nick carry his too.

Chapter 5
Crossing the Line

BY EARLY AFTERNOON, the heat had settled heavily over the city. Nick walked slowly down his street, each step feeling harder than the last. He had only been away from home for a matter of hours, but somehow it already felt like another life.

His stomach tightened as the house came into view. He slowed near the sidewalk, staring at it as if it might swallow him whole the moment he got too close. Part of him wanted to turn around and keep walking until the entire street disappeared behind him, but he couldn't leave without his things. More than that, he couldn't leave without seeing his mom.

Nick stepped up to the front door and stood there, his hand hovering over the knob. His heart pounded so hard it felt painful. He closed his eyes for a second, trying to steady himself, then finally turned the handle and pushed the door open.

The smell hit him first—alcohol, stale smoke, and something sour that seemed soaked into the walls. His chest tightened immediately. He stepped inside as quietly as he could, but before he had gone more than a few feet, he heard shouting from deeper in the house.

Nick moved toward the kitchen, each step pulling him toward something he already knew he didn't want to see. When he reached the doorway, he froze.

Broken plates littered the floor. Glass glittered across the tile. Pots and pans were scattered everywhere, and in the middle of it all stood his father, gripping a pan in one hand and towering over Nick's mother. A bruise was already forming along her cheek, and tears streaked down her face as she whispered apologies that were not hers to make.

Something in Nick broke loose.

He didn't stop to think. He grabbed the nearest pot and swung with everything he had. The metal connected with a sickening crack, and his father dropped to the floor instantly, his body hitting the tile with a heavy thud.

For half a second, the room went silent.

Then Nick rushed to his mother and helped her to her feet. His hands were shaking so badly he could barely hold onto her, but he managed to guide her toward the stairs. They didn't stop until they were inside his bedroom with the door slammed shut behind them.

From downstairs came a groan, followed by movement.

Then his father's voice tore through the house.

"Boy! Where the fuck are you?"

Nick shoved his dresser against the bedroom door just as the pounding began. The wood rattled under each hit, the frame shaking harder every time his father slammed against it. Nick grabbed an ice pack from the small freezer in his room and pressed it carefully against his mother's cheek while she winced and held it in place.

"Mom," he said, his voice breaking, "are you okay?"

She nodded weakly, but he could see she was struggling. "I'll be all right."

"No," Nick said, shaking his head. "No, this isn't all right. You can't stay here. Come with me. Please. I've got somewhere we can go."

Her eyes filled with tears, and for a moment she just looked at him, as if trying to memorize his face. "I can't," she whispered.

"Mom—"

"He'll find us," she said, gripping his hands tightly. "You don't understand. He'll find us."

"I don't care," Nick said. "I'm not leaving you here with him."

"You have to."

The words hit him harder than anything else. The pounding on the door grew louder, followed by his father's furious shouting, but for a moment all Nick could hear was her voice.

"You have to go," she said again, stronger this time. "You have a chance to get out. Don't waste it."

Nick shook his head as tears spilled down his face. "I can't just leave you."

"You can," she said, squeezing his hands tighter. "And you will."

Another violent crash shook the door. Nick flinched, and his mother leaned closer, her voice turning urgent.

"Listen to me. You go. You get out of here. You build a life. That's what matters now."

"I'll come back," Nick said. "I swear I'll come back for you."

"I know you will," she replied softly. "But not today."

When the pounding started again, even harder than before, she looked toward the door and then back at him. "Now go," she said. "Please."

Nick hesitated only a second longer. Then he moved as fast as he could, throwing clothes, money, and a few personal things into a bag. His breathing was ragged, and his hands shook so badly he nearly dropped everything he touched.

At the window, he stopped and turned back.

"I love you," he said.

"I love you too," she answered, her voice breaking.

Nick climbed out and dropped to the ground below. He didn't stop running until the house was far behind him and his lungs burned from the effort.

Later that afternoon, Ryan stood outside his car with a coffee in hand, scanning the street while he waited. He had arrived too early, but he hadn't been able to help it. The last twenty-four hours had already changed more in his life than he could fully process, and now he was about to bring someone he barely knew into his home.

Strangely, it didn't feel reckless.

It felt necessary.

When Nick appeared at the far end of the street, Ryan straightened without even realizing he was doing it. Nick looked exhausted, but there was relief in his expression too, as if simply making it there had taken more strength than Ryan could imagine.

"Hey," Nick said as he came closer.

"Hey," Ryan replied. He held up the iced coffee. "I got you something. Caramel. Hope that's okay."

Nick smiled faintly. "Yeah, that's perfect. Thanks."

They got into the car and pulled away from the curb. For the first several minutes, neither of them spoke. The city rolled by in a blur of storefronts, traffic lights, and shimmering afternoon heat, and despite the beauty of the day, something heavy sat between them.

Ryan finally broke the silence.

"How did things go at home?"

Nick looked out the window before answering. "Not good."

Ryan kept his eyes on the road. "I figured."

Nick let out a quiet breath, then said, "I had to leave. I didn't really have a choice."

Ryan's grip tightened slightly on the steering wheel. "I'm sorry."

Nick shrugged, but there was nothing casual in the movement. "My mom told me to go. Said it was the only way."

Ryan glanced over at him. "You did what you had to do."

For a moment, Nick didn't respond. When he finally did, his voice had gone softer. "I just hope she's okay."

Ryan didn't have anything comforting enough to offer, so he told the truth as gently as he could. "You're safe now. That matters."

Nick nodded, though the tension in his shoulders didn't fully ease. Ryan could tell there was more he wanted to say, but he also knew better than to push. Some stories came out only when they were ready.

By the time they reached Ryan's house, the smell of grilling drifted through the warm air. Nick stepped out of the car slowly and took in the house, the yard, the clean lines of the patio, and the easy light spilling from the windows. For a second, he just stood there, as if none of it felt real.

Ryan led him inside and out toward the back patio where his family was setting up dinner. "Hey," Ryan called. "We're here. This is Nick."

Ryan's mom turned with a warm smile that immediately softened the moment. "Hi, Nick. It's so nice to meet you. You're more than welcome here. Make yourself at home."

Nick blinked, clearly caught off guard by how genuine she sounded. "Thank you. I really appreciate it."

"Why don't you boys go get settled?" she said. "Dinner's almost ready."

Ryan nodded and led Nick upstairs to the guest room. It was spacious, clean, and comfortable, with a neatly made bed, a dresser, a desk, and an attached bathroom. Nick stepped inside slowly, taking in every detail as if he didn't quite trust what he was seeing.

Ryan stayed near the doorway, giving him space. "This is your room," he said. "Take your time. Come down whenever you're ready."

Nick nodded without looking at him. "Thanks."

When Ryan left, Nick sat down on the edge of the bed, and the weight of everything that had happened finally crashed into him. He buried his face in his hands and cried, not out of fear this time, but out of sheer release. After a few minutes, he wiped his face, stood up, and headed downstairs.

Dinner was warm and easy in a way that felt almost unreal to Nick. Ryan's family welcomed him without hesitation, including him in the conversation as if he had always belonged there. There was laughter at the table, casual teasing, and the kind of comfort that comes from people who feel safe with one another.

For the first time in a long time, Nick felt something unfamiliar growing inside him.

He felt safe.

After dinner, they cleaned up together and headed upstairs. Ryan dropped onto his bed with a tired sigh while Nick leaned back in a chair and looked up at the ceiling.

"You have a really great family," Nick said quietly.

Ryan gave a small shrug. "Yeah, I guess I do."

Nick turned to look at him. "No. You really do."

Ryan looked back at him and understood immediately that Nick wasn't just complimenting them. He was mourning the fact that he had never had that for himself.

"You've got one too," Ryan said, though even he knew the words came out thinner than he intended.

Nick didn't answer right away. After a pause, he said, "Maybe someday."

Later that night, Nick returned to his room and closed the door gently behind him. He stood there in the quiet for a long moment, taking it all in again—the soft light, the clean sheets, the silence that did not carry fear inside it.

Then he slid down to the floor and cried again.

This time, though, relief was stronger than grief.

When he finally climbed into bed, he realized it had been years since he had fallen asleep in a place that felt even remotely like home. Outside, the sky stretched wide and clear above the house, stars scattered across the dark.

As the night slowly gave way to morning once again, the world still felt uncertain, but it no longer felt completely closed.

For the first time in a very long while, it felt possible.

Chapter 6
Over the Rainbow

THE HOUSE WAS QUIET when the morning began, the kind of quiet that felt warm instead of empty. Sunlight filtered through the windows and settled gently across the kitchen.

Ryan woke just after nine and lay there for a moment, staring at the ceiling. Everything from the night before still sat with him—the conversation, the realization, the feeling that something inside him had shifted in a way he couldn't undo. It didn't feel like a phase or a passing thought anymore. It felt like the beginning of something.

He finally got up and headed downstairs, drawn by the smell of coffee. In the kitchen, his mom and sister were already moving around, plates clinking softly as they finished breakfast. Ryan stepped in and stopped when he saw Nick already there, sitting at the breakfast bar, relaxed, drinking coffee like he'd been part of the house for years.

That caught him off guard.

"Good morning," Ryan said, grabbing a mug. "I'm surprised you're up. I figured you'd be dead asleep."

Nick smiled. "Couldn't sleep. Your mom was already up, so we started talking."

"Well," Ryan said, pouring coffee, "that explains why it smells amazing in here."

His mom turned, smiling warmly as she set plates down. "I made enough for both of you. Eat."

"Thanks, Mom."

Nick looked at her, sincere. "Thank you. Really."

She gave him a look that was equal parts kindness and certainty. "Around here, we take care of people. You're welcome as long as you need to be."

Ryan noticed the way Nick's expression shifted—just slightly, but enough to matter.

After breakfast, the house quieted again once his mom and sister left. Ryan leaned back against the counter and looked over at Nick.

"So. What do you want to do today?"

Nick didn't hesitate. "We're getting you new clothes."

Ryan raised an eyebrow. "We are?"

"Yes," Nick said, already smiling. "Because what you have now? That's not going to work tonight."

"What's wrong with what I have?"

"It's great," Nick said. "If you're going to a country club."

Ryan laughed. "Wow."

"I'm serious," Nick continued. "You don't need to go crazy—but something that actually shows you off? Yeah. We're doing that."

Ryan considered it. A few days ago, he would have shut that idea down instantly. Now it didn't seem nearly as impossible as it should have.

"Okay," he said. "Let's do it."

By midday, they were driving toward South Beach with the top down, music blasting, and the sun high overhead. The air was thick with heat, but everything felt alive. Nick sang along without hesitation, loud and completely unbothered, and Ryan found himself laughing more than he expected.

It felt easy.

Too easy for how new all of this was.

When they stepped into the crowded streets, the energy hit immediately—music spilling out of storefronts, people moving in every direction, color everywhere. Nick stopped in front of a boutique and turned to Ryan.

"This one."

Ryan eyed it. It was nothing like the places he normally shopped.

"Trust me," Nick said.

Ryan sighed. "All right."

Inside, the store was bold—bright colors, fitted cuts, pieces that were meant to be seen. Before Ryan could fully take it in, Nick was already calling out to someone near the back.

"Ricardo!"

A man turned and lit up instantly. "Well, look who it is. And who is this?"

Nick gestured toward Ryan. "This is Ryan. He's new."

Ricardo's eyes moved over Ryan quickly, assessing but not judging. "Oh," he said, smiling. "Yes. We can work with this."

Ryan wasn't sure whether to laugh or brace himself.

An hour later, he stood in front of a mirror, barely recognizing himself. The shirt was more fitted, slightly sheer under the light, paired with darker, tailored pants that sat just right. It wasn't over-the-top, but it was confident. Different.

Nick stepped beside him. "There he is."

Ryan stared at his reflection. "This is… a lot."

"It's exactly enough."

Ryan looked again. Same face. Same person. But something about him looked less guarded, less careful, and he didn't hate it.

That night, everything changed again.

The city lit up, music spilling into the streets as people moved with purpose toward wherever the night would take them. Ryan stood outside the club with his heart pounding.

"Over the Rainbow," Nick said, glancing at him. "Ready?"

Ryan exhaled. "Yeah. I think so."

They stepped inside, and everything hit at once—music, lights, color, bodies moving shoulder to shoulder, laughter, energy. Ryan stopped just inside the entrance, taking it all in.

Nick leaned closer. "You good?"

Ryan nodded slowly. "Yeah. Just… wow."

Because it was.

It wasn't just a club. It was something else entirely. People weren't watching themselves here. They weren't holding back. They were just being.

Nick started greeting people almost immediately—hugs, laughter, familiarity everywhere.

"Hey! There he is!" someone called.

A man approached with his arms open. "You disappeared on me!"

Nick laughed. "I've been busy."

Then he turned. "This is Ryan."

The man—Dan—smiled warmly. "Welcome. First time?"

Ryan nodded. "Yeah."

"Well," Dan said, "you picked the right place. This is family here."

And somehow, he meant it.

Ryan could see it, too. People were greeting Nick like he mattered. Like they were glad he'd come back. No one was sizing him up or making him prove himself. They just folded him right in, and the shift in Nick was impossible to miss. He stood straighter. He smiled easier. He looked more alive here than Ryan had ever seen him.

That was when Ryan understood this place meant much more to Nick than a fun night out.

The show started soon after. The lights dropped, the music surged, and the room erupted. The first performer stepped onto the stage with flawless makeup, towering presence, and complete control of the room. The crowd went wild instantly.

Ryan stared, completely caught off guard.

It wasn't just performance. It was transformation—confidence, precision, art.

The next act hit harder. Then another. Each one was bigger, louder, and more alive than the last. The drag queens didn't just perform songs; they owned them. One came out in a full Madonna-inspired look, moving like she'd stepped straight out of a music video. Another had a Britney outfit so exact it made Ryan laugh in disbelief. The makeup, wigs, costumes, gestures, and attitude all worked together in a way he never could have imagined until he saw it in person.

Nick was singing along beside him, completely in it, smiling wider than Ryan had ever seen. Watching him, Ryan began to understand something he hadn't fully grasped before. This wasn't just entertainment for Nick. This was where he got to breathe. Where he wasn't judged. Where he wasn't afraid.

This was his family.

As the show went on, Ryan found himself getting pulled in deeper and deeper. At first, he had only been watching in stunned fascination, but after a while the shock gave way to admiration. He could see the work in it, the discipline, the nerve it took to get up there and turn yourself into something bigger than yourself for the crowd. It was wild, funny, sexy, theatrical, and somehow heartfelt all at once.

Then everything shifted again.

"Ladies and gentlemen—and everyone in between," one of the performers called, scanning the crowd, "we've got a new face in the house tonight."

Ryan froze.

"No—no, no," he muttered.

Nick was already laughing. "Oh, this is happening."

"Ryan!" the performer called. "Get up here!"

The crowd started cheering.

Ryan hesitated, but hands were already on his shoulders, people encouraging him, pulling him forward—not forcing, just lifting him into it. Next thing he knew, he was on stage under hot lights with his heart racing so hard he thought it might crack through his ribs.

"Don't worry," one of the queens said quietly. "Just have fun."

The music started. At first, he froze. Then the crowd cheered again, and something in him loosened.

He moved—awkward at first, off-beat and uncertain—but he didn't stop. And the crowd didn't care. They loved it. They clapped, cheered, and hyped him up like he'd been doing it for years. Instead of judging him, they carried him through it.

By the time the song ended, he was laughing, breathless, adrenaline rushing through him. He even managed a dramatic little turn at the end that made the room cheer louder. The applause hit him like a wave—not pressure, not judgment, just acceptance.

Something about the moment felt bigger than the performance itself.

It felt like a door opening.

When he came offstage, people were congratulating him, slapping him on the shoulder, laughing with him instead of at him. A couple of Nick's friends hugged him like he'd just passed some kind of initiation.

"You did great, babe," one of the queens said. "Messy, but great."

Ryan laughed. "That feels fair."

Nick was grinning at him like he'd known all along this would happen.

Later, once the music had softened and the crowd had thinned a little, Ryan stood outside with Nick in the cooler air, the noise of the club fading behind them. The adrenaline had settled into something quieter now, but it was still there.

"That was…" Ryan started, then laughed. "I don't even have words."

Nick smiled. "You don't need them."

Ryan looked back toward the entrance, the music still pulsing faintly from inside. "I think something changed tonight."

Nick looked at him, more serious now. "Yeah," he said quietly. "It usually does."

Ryan understood then what that place really was.

Not just a club.

A refuge. A beginning. And maybe, for people like Nick, the closest thing to home they'd ever had.

They stayed longer than Ryan expected, talking, laughing, and taking in the rest of the night. For once, he wasn't trying to pin anything down or explain it away.

He just let the feeling exist.

And for the first time in his life, it felt right.

Chapter 7
Something Begins to Shift

THE MORNING MOVED ALONG QUICKLY, and about an hour after Ryan and Nick returned home, the rest of the family came back as well. The front door opened to the sound of grocery bags rustling and voices carrying in from the driveway. It had clearly been a busy morning for them.

Ryan came downstairs just as they were unloading everything onto the kitchen counters.

"Good morning, honey," his mom said, glancing over her shoulder. "How was your night? Do anything exciting?"

Ryan leaned casually against the counter. "It was good. Really fun. We didn't do a whole lot—just hung out, went out for a bit. Nothing too crazy. Pretty chill."

"Well, that sounds nice," she said, setting a bag down. "Nick had a good time too?"

"Yeah," Ryan said. "I think he did. He's still upstairs. Probably catching up on sleep."

His mom nodded. "We were thinking about dinner tonight. Maybe sushi or Chinese. Not sure what he likes, though. What do you think?"

Ryan shrugged. "Sushi sounds good. I'll ask him when he wakes up."

"Perfect. Not until later, though. Maybe after five. It's almost noon now," she added. "We might spend some time out by the pool first."

Ryan smiled. "That sounds like a plan."

His sister popped into the room. "Pool?"

Ryan pointed at her. "You read my mind."

Within minutes, they had all scattered—Ryan and his sister heading upstairs to change while his parents finished putting groceries away. The day had turned hot and bright, the kind of summer heat that practically pulled you toward the water.

Soon enough, Ryan and his sister were in the pool, splashing, laughing, and trying to cool off under the sun. His parents joined them shortly after, and for a while, everything felt easy and uncomplicated. They floated, joked, and soaked in the warmth of the day; the kind of simple moment most people don't realize they'll miss someday.

Upstairs, Nick stirred awake slowly, listening before he even opened his eyes. He could hear faint splashes and laughter drifting in through the windows, and the sound alone made him smile. It took him a second to remember where he was, and when he did, the feeling that followed was almost overwhelming.

He sat up, running a hand through his hair, still groggy. The quiet comfort of the room, the sunlight, the distant sounds of a family enjoying the day—it all felt surreal, like something he wasn't supposed to have but somehow did.

He changed into swim trunks, grabbed a water bottle from the fridge, and stepped out onto the lanai. The moment he saw them in the pool, something settled in his chest—something warm and unfamiliar, but undeniably good.

"Hey," he called out. "I heard all the noise and figured I'd join."

Ryan looked over immediately, smiling. "There he is."

His mom added, "Perfect timing. We were just talking about dinner. Sushi tonight—does that work for you?"

Nick nodded quickly. "Yeah, absolutely. I'd love that."

"Good," she said. "Go ahead and jump in. I'll put together some snacks for later."

Nick stepped into the pool, letting the water wash over him. It was warm, refreshing, and grounding all at once. For a while, he didn't say much—just swam, floated, and let himself exist in the moment.

After some time, they drifted out of the pool, grabbing towels and moving toward the shaded seating area. Ryan's mom brought out a spread of snacks—cheese, crackers, chips, and fruit—and everyone gathered around casually, eating and talking without any structure or pressure.

Nick sat with them, laughing, listening, occasionally adding to the conversation. It felt so natural that it almost scared him. This wasn't his life, and yet, for now, it was.

Ryan eventually settled into a chair beside him. "You enjoying the day so far?"

Nick nodded. "Yeah. It's been really great. Honestly… I can't remember the last time I had a day like this."

Ryan leaned back, stretching out his legs. "I'm glad you're here."

Nick hesitated for just a second before responding. "Your family… they're amazing. I don't think you realize how lucky you are."

Ryan glanced over at him, softer now. "Yeah," he said quietly. "I do."

The conversation faded after that, but the silence that followed wasn't empty. It carried something unspoken between them—something neither of them was ready to define yet.

As the afternoon wore on, Ryan's parents and sister headed inside to start getting ready for dinner, leaving Nick sitting near the edge of the pool with his feet in the water. Ryan stayed behind a little longer, stretched out in the sun with his eyes closed.

For a moment, everything felt perfect. The warmth, the quiet, the sense of belonging—it all settled over him like something he had always known but never truly noticed.

And still, something lingered beneath it.

A feeling he couldn't quite name.

He sat up, pushing it aside for now, and looked over at Nick. "You heading in?"

"Yeah," Nick said. "In a minute."

Ryan nodded. "I'll see you inside."

Dinner that night felt like stepping into another world for Nick. The restaurant was beautiful—soft lighting, polished wood, quiet conversations filling the space—and for a moment, he felt completely out of place.

But that feeling didn't last.

Ryan's family made sure of that.

They talked, laughed, ordered food together, and before long, Nick found himself relaxing into the experience instead of questioning it. When the food arrived, everyone shared dishes, passing things around, encouraging him to try new things.

Ryan's dad leaned forward slightly at one point. "You know you're welcome to stay with us as long as you need."

Nick blinked, caught off guard. "Thank you. That… really means a lot."

"And we mean it," his mom added. "You're family here."

For a moment, Nick didn't trust himself to speak. He nodded instead, hoping that was enough to convey how much those words meant.

The rest of the dinner passed in a blur of conversation and laughter. By the time they left, Nick felt something he hadn't felt in a long time—something steady and real.

The ride home was quieter, but comfortable. Music played softly, and the glow of the evening lingered in the air. Nick sat in the backseat beside Ryan's sister, laughing with her about something small, while Ryan watched them in the rearview mirror, smiling to himself.

Everything felt right.

But beneath that, something was shifting.

Later that night, after everyone had gone to their rooms, Ryan lay on his bed staring at the ceiling. He wasn't tired—not really. His mind kept circling back to the day, to dinner, to the way everything felt just slightly different now.

A knock at the door broke his thoughts.

He got up and opened it to find Nick standing there.

"Hey," Nick said. "You want to hang out for a bit? Watch something?"

Ryan smiled. "Yeah. Come in."

They settled onto the bed, scrolling through movies until they landed on *American Beauty*. It felt like an easy choice, something familiar enough to relax into but still interesting enough to hold their attention.

As the movie played, they leaned slightly toward each other without realizing it. Nick laughed at certain moments, nudging Ryan lightly, pointing things out. The contact was casual, natural, but Ryan noticed it.

It wasn't uncomfortable.

It was just new.

By the time the movie ended, it was well past midnight. The room had gone quiet again, the kind of quiet that follows something meaningful.

Nick stood near the door, hesitating for a moment before speaking.

"Hey… I just wanted to say thanks. For everything. Today, last night—all of it."

Ryan smiled. "Anytime. I've really enjoyed it too."

Nick stepped closer, leaning in for what was clearly meant to be a simple hug. Their timing was off by just enough, and instead of a hug—

Their lips met.

For a split second, both of them froze. Ryan didn't pull away immediately, and neither did Nick. The moment hung there, uncertain and charged, neither of them quite ready to break it.

Then Nick pulled back abruptly.

"I'm sorry," he said quickly, his voice tight. "I didn't mean to—good night."

He turned and left before Ryan could respond.

Ryan stood there for a moment, still processing what had just happened. Then, slowly, a small smile crept across his face as he sat back down on the bed and leaned against the headboard.

This time, when he stared up at the ceiling, he wasn't searching for what was missing.

Because something had just changed.

Chapter 8
The Morning After

THE NIGHT STRETCHED ON far longer than it should have, quiet in a way that made sleep nearly impossible. Nick lay in bed staring at the ceiling, replaying the moment over and over again.

The kiss.

He turned onto his side, then onto his back again, restless. His thoughts wouldn't settle. What had he done? What was Ryan thinking? Had he ruined everything before anything even had the chance to begin?

He squeezed his eyes shut, trying to make sense of it, but there was only one explanation that kept coming back. He liked him more than he had planned to, and probably more than he should. The worst part was that he hadn't hated it, not even a little.

A small, guilty smile crept across his face despite himself. Ryan had kissed him back. Not for long, not fully, but enough to make everything more complicated.

Across the hall, Ryan hadn't slept much better. He had dozed off for a few hours, but when he woke up, the memory came back immediately. The kiss lingered in his mind in a way he hadn't expected. It was different—completely different from anything he had experienced before—but not in a bad way.

He lay there staring at the ceiling, trying to sort through what he felt. There was excitement, curiosity, and something else he couldn't quite name yet. Was this what had been missing?

He exhaled slowly and ran a hand through his hair. He didn't know what Nick had been thinking when it happened, and he wasn't sure he was ready to ask. Not yet. Not when everything still felt so new. But one thing was clear: he hadn't wanted it to stop.

By the time the morning light crept fully into the room, neither of them had really rested. The house was still quiet, the early hour giving them both space to think.

Ryan reached for his phone and noticed a message waiting.

Jim.

How you been? Haven't heard from you, dude. What the fuck has been going on?

Ryan stared at the screen for a moment, realizing just how much he had pulled away over the last few days. Everything had changed so quickly that he hadn't even stopped to think about how it looked from the outside. After a moment, he typed back:

Hey, sorry. Been laying low after the other night. I'm good though. We should catch up soon.

He set his phone down again, unsure what that "soon" really meant.

Upstairs, Nick had already given up on trying to sleep. He splashed water on his face, hoping it would clear his head, but it didn't do much. The thoughts were still there—about Ryan, about the kiss, and about what came next.

He needed air.

He changed quickly and slipped out of the house, stepping into the quiet morning. The neighborhood was still and peaceful, the kind of calm he wasn't used to. No shouting, no tension, no fear of what might be waiting around the corner.

Just silence.

He walked slowly, letting the rhythm of his steps ground him. The houses were beautiful and well-kept, everything in its place. It felt like a completely different world from the one he came from. For a few minutes, he let himself enjoy it and simply exist inside that quiet.

By the time he turned back toward the house, he felt lighter, at least a little.

When he stepped inside, he heard movement in the kitchen. Ryan. Nick paused in the doorway for a second before stepping in. Ryan was focused on making coffee, completely unaware he wasn't alone.

Ryan turned suddenly. "Oh—shit. I didn't see you there."

Nick gave a small smile. "I just got back. Didn't want to interrupt."

Ryan nodded, a little awkward but trying to play it off. "Yeah… no, you're good. How are you this morning?"

"Better," Nick said. "Went for a walk. It's really nice out there."

"Yeah, it is."

There was a brief pause, just long enough for both of them to feel it. They were both avoiding the same thing. The kiss hung in the air between them, unspoken but impossible to ignore.

Ryan poured two cups of coffee and handed one to Nick. "You want to sit outside?"

"Yeah," Nick said. "That sounds good."

They stepped out onto the lanai and settled into chairs with their coffee. The morning was already warm, the air thick with humidity, but still peaceful. Nick leaned back and stared out at the yard.

"You ever think about how easy things would be if people could just… be themselves? No hiding. No worrying about what anyone thinks?"

Ryan let out a quiet breath. "Yeah. All the time."

They sat with that for a moment, and then the conversation shifted. It moved through lighter topics first—running, school, future plans—but, as it always seemed to, it circled back to life, identity, and what came next.

Eventually, Ryan looked over at him.

"So… about last night."

Nick froze slightly, his grip tightening around his coffee mug.

Ryan continued carefully. "I wasn't expecting that."

Nick let out a breath, half nervous and half embarrassed. "Yeah. Me neither."

A beat passed between them. Then Ryan smiled a little.

"I didn't hate it," he said. "Actually… I liked it."

That was all it took to ease the tension. Nick let out a small laugh and shook his head.

"Well… that's good. Because I was freaking out."

"Yeah," Ryan said, smiling now. "I could tell."

They both laughed quietly, and the awkwardness finally loosened. Neither of them tried to define what had happened, but both of them knew something had shifted.

Later that morning, after breakfast and a slow start to the day, Ryan checked his phone again. Jim had replied.

Meet me by the beach. I'm working.

Ryan stared at the message, then glanced at Nick. "You want to come with me? Go see a friend?"

Nick nodded. "Yeah. I'm in."

The drive was quiet, both of them lost in their own thoughts. Ryan wasn't sure what to expect, and part of him still wasn't ready—but he knew he couldn't avoid it forever.

When they arrived, Jim was already there.

"Sup, man?" Jim said, giving Ryan a quick fist bump.

"Hey," Ryan replied. "This is Nick."

They exchanged quick greetings before grabbing drinks and sitting down. Jim didn't waste time.

"Dude, what happened to you? You just disappeared."

Ryan leaned back slightly. "I needed space. That night was… a lot."

Jim nodded. "Yeah. I figured."

There was a pause. Ryan took a breath.

"There's something I need to tell you."

Jim looked at him, waiting.

Ryan didn't hesitate this time.

"I'm gay."

Jim blinked, clearly thrown off. "Wait—what?"

"I'm gay," Ryan repeated. "I like guys."

Jim sat back, processing, his expression shifting from confusion to something harder to read. "And… you figured this out with him?" he asked, nodding toward Nick.

Ryan frowned slightly. "No. I figured it out myself. He just helped me understand it."

Jim shook his head and stood up. "Man… I don't even know what to say right now."

"Then don't leave," Ryan said. "Just sit and talk to me."

"I can't," Jim replied quickly. "I gotta get back to work."

"Jim—"

But he was already walking away.

Ryan sat there stunned, staring after him. Nick stayed quiet for a moment before speaking gently.

"I'm sorry. I didn't mean to come between you guys."

Ryan shook his head unsure how to process Jim's reaction. "You didn't. He just… needs time, I guess."

"Yeah," Nick said. "Some people do."

They sat there a moment longer before heading down to the beach. The sun was high now, the sand warm beneath their feet as they laid out their towels.

Ryan leaned back and stared up at the sky. "I knew it might go like that," he said quietly. "Still sucks."

Nick turned his head toward him. "If he's a real friend, he'll come around."

Ryan nodded slowly. "I hope so."

They lay there in silence for a while, letting the sun wash over them, until a voice cut through the moment.

"Nick?"

Nick sat up quickly and lowered his sunglasses. His expression changed instantly—shock, recognition, and something deeper that Ryan couldn't quite place. He looked toward the voice and swallowed.

"Uh… hi."

Ryan pushed himself up on his elbows and looked between them. He didn't know who the guy was yet, but something in Nick's face told him more than words would have. This wasn't just some random person from the beach, and whatever history stood between them, it wasn't going to be simple.

Chapter 9
Unfinished Business

SOMETHING ABOUT NICK'S REACTION FELT OFF, and Ryan noticed it right away. The moment that guy said his name, everything shifted. Nick's expression tightened, his posture changed, and whatever ease had been there just disappeared.

Ryan didn't know who this guy was yet, but he knew one thing—this wasn't just some random person. This was history, and not the good kind.

Ryan studied him quietly. The guy who had called out to Nick wasn't alone. Another man stood just slightly behind and to his side, relaxed but observant, like he already knew this interaction had layers to it.

Both of them were hard to ignore. The one addressing Nick had a presence that pulled attention without effort. Tall, athletic, confident in a way that didn't need to try. Gold chain, bracelet, expensive sunglasses—the kind of guy people noticed whether they meant to or not. The other guy was equally put together, though quieter, watching the exchange with calm curiosity.

Ryan clocked all of it in seconds, but his focus stayed on Nick. He looked like he'd just been pulled into something he didn't want to face, and there was tension in the air before anyone even spoke.

"Hey, Gabriel," Nick finally said, trying to sound normal. "How are you?"

"Good," Gabriel replied, holding his gaze. "How about you, Nick?"

The way they looked at each other said everything. There was history there—unfinished, complicated, and heavy.

Nick didn't ease into it. "I'm good. Didn't expect to see you here. Thought you were in L.A. Didn't work out?"

Gabriel gave a small smirk. "It worked out. I'm just back visiting for a bit. Life's good there."

Nick nodded, but his eyes flicked to the guy standing next to him.

"This is Matt," Gabriel said. "Friend from L.A."

They exchanged quick greetings, and Nick gestured toward Ryan.

"This is Ryan."

Ryan stepped in with an easy smile. "Hey, man."

For a brief second, everything felt normal. Then it shifted again.

Gabriel looked back at Nick. "So… how's life? Still in the same place?"

Nick's jaw tightened slightly. "No. I got out. I'm staying with Ryan now."

Gabriel nodded slowly. "Yeah… you never really liked talking about home."

That was all it took. Nick's tone sharpened.

"Yeah. There's a reason for that."

The tension built fast after that. It didn't explode, but it simmered—old resentment creeping in, things left unsaid pushing their way to the surface. Years of silence sat heavy between them.

Gabriel didn't fight it. "I messed up," he said quietly. "I know I did."

Nick let out a short breath, almost a laugh, but there was no humor in it. "Yeah," he said. "You did."

The air between them felt thick and uncomfortable, like neither of them knew how to stand in it. After a moment, Gabriel shifted.

"I'll let you guys get back to your day. But I'm performing tonight. You should come."

Nick hesitated, and Ryan saw it immediately. He didn't want to. But Ryan spoke before he could stop himself.

"Yeah, we'll be there."

Nick shot him a look, but it was too late.

Gabriel smiled. "Cool. I'll see you guys tonight."

They didn't say anything at first after Gabriel walked away. Nick just sat there for a second before exhaling.

"I was trying to avoid him," he said.

Ryan leaned back in the sand. "I get that. But maybe this is your chance to finish it."

Nick didn't answer right away. He stared out toward the water, thinking it over, then finally nodded.

"Yeah," he said quietly. "Maybe."

The rest of the afternoon felt different—lighter on the surface, but with something unsettled underneath. The plan was set. They were going tonight.

Back at the house, they split up to get ready. Ryan tried not to overthink it, but his mind kept circling back to the same thought: that wasn't just a friendship. Whatever happened between Nick and Gabriel, it was more.

Upstairs, Nick stood in front of the mirror, working the dye through his hair. He wasn't just getting ready; he was gearing up. By the time he rinsed it out, the color came through bold and bright—red, sharp, impossible to ignore.

Perfect. He wanted Gabriel to notice.

His phone buzzed with a message from Gabriel.

We need to talk tonight. You deserve to know everything.

Nick stared at the screen, jaw tightening. "Yeah," he muttered. "We do."

He didn't respond.

Later, when Nick came downstairs, Ryan blinked.

"Whoa," he said. "Okay… that looks really good."

Nick smirked. "That's the goal."

Ryan tilted his head. "Trying to make a statement?"

Nick didn't hesitate. "Absolutely."

Ryan laughed. "Well, mission accomplished."

The club was already alive when they got there. Music pulsed through the room, lights flashing, people gathering near the stage. Nick slipped right into it, greeting friends, laughing, completely at ease.

Ryan noticed it instantly. This was Nick's world, and he looked completely at home in it.

When the show started, the energy shifted again. Gabriel and Matt took the stage, and the crowd reacted immediately. The performance was confident, controlled, and undeniably hot. Their routine leaned harder into sex appeal than the drag show Ryan had seen before, and the room ate it up.

Even Ryan had to admit it.

"Okay… yeah," he said under his breath. "They're good."

Nick didn't answer, but he didn't look away either. Ryan could tell he was watching for more than the performance. He was watching Gabriel himself—the way he moved, the way people reacted to him, the way he still knew exactly how to command a room.

After the show, Nick didn't stick around long.

"I'll be back," he said, already heading toward backstage.

Ryan watched him go, knowing exactly what this was.

Backstage, everything felt quieter and heavier. Nick stepped inside, and for a moment, neither of them spoke. Gabriel had already started changing out of part of his costume, the performance polish still hanging around him. Up close, though, the swagger from the stage looked thinner. Less effortless.

Nick crossed his arms. "Can Matt give us a minute?"

Matt looked from one to the other, clearly reading the mood. "Yeah," he said. "I'll step out."

The door shut behind him.

The silence that followed was worse than shouting. Nick stared at Gabriel for several long seconds before he finally spoke.

"So what is it you really want?"

Gabriel didn't dodge it. "I wanted to see you. And I wanted to say what I should've said a long time ago."

Nick let out a bitter laugh. "You're a little late."

"I know."

Nick shook his head. "No, Gabriel. You don't get to do that. You don't get to come back in here looking all polished and sorry and act like time didn't happen."

Gabriel swallowed but didn't interrupt.

Nick stepped closer. "You told them I wasn't your boyfriend."

Gabriel's expression shifted instantly. "I panicked. They weren't safe, Nick. I thought—"

"You thought what?" Nick snapped. "That humiliating me in front of everybody was protecting me? That standing there and acting like I was some nobody hanging around you was supposed to make it better?"

Gabriel's voice dropped. "I was scared."

"You left me," Nick cut in. "That's what you did."

The words landed hard between them.

Nick's breathing turned uneven, anger and hurt colliding all at once. "You stood there and let me take that by myself. Then you ran to L.A. like I was just something embarrassing you wanted to forget."

"That's not what you were."

"Then what was I?" Nick shot back. "Because from where I was standing, I looked pretty damn disposable."

Gabriel looked away for a second, then back at him. "You weren't disposable. I was a coward."

Nick's eyes filled, but his voice only sharpened. "You said I wasn't your boyfriend, Gabriel. Do you have any idea what that did to me? I was already dealing with shit at home. I already felt like I didn't matter anywhere. And then the one person I thought actually saw me acted like I was nothing."

Gabriel took a step forward. "I never thought you were nothing."

"Well, you were real convincing."

The room went still.

Gabriel dragged a hand over his face. "I hated myself after that."

Nick laughed again, bitter and wounded. "Good."

"I deserve that."

"Yeah. You do."

Gabriel stared at him, and when he spoke again, the performance was gone completely. "I loved you, Nick."

That hit harder than Nick expected. It showed all over his face.

He looked down, then away, then back at him. "Don't do that."

"I'm not trying to manipulate you."

"Then what are you trying to do?"

"I'm trying to tell the truth for once."

Nick's voice cracked. "That truth would've been useful years ago."

Gabriel didn't argue. "I know."

Nick wiped angrily at his eyes. "Do you have any idea how long I hated you?"

Gabriel answered without hesitation. "Probably not as long as I hated myself."

Nick shook his head. "I waited for you. For a while, I actually waited. I kept thinking maybe you'd call, maybe you'd come back, maybe you'd explain something. Then I saw you out with all your new friends acting like you didn't even know me. That was worse than the breakup. That made me feel stupid."

Gabriel's face tightened. "I froze. That's not an excuse. I just… I didn't know how to come back from what I'd done."

"You could've started with not pretending I never existed."

"I know."

"You say that a lot."

"Because it's true."

Nick looked at him for a long moment, chest rising and falling fast. The anger was still there, but now it was tangled up with grief, old love, humiliation, and the part of him that had once wanted Gabriel to choose him openly.

Gabriel stepped closer again, slower this time, giving Nick space to pull away if he wanted.

"I am sorry," he said quietly. "Not in some cheap way. Not because I ran into you and suddenly feel bad. I've been sorry. I just wasn't brave enough to face you."

Nick's mouth tightened. "You weren't brave enough back then either."

"No," Gabriel said. "I wasn't."

For a second, neither of them moved. Then Gabriel reached up carefully and wiped a tear from Nick's cheek. Nick let him.

That only made the whole thing worse.

Gabriel pulled him into a hug, and Nick stood stiff for half a second before giving in and clutching the back of his shirt. The sob that came out of him sounded like years of anger finally breaking open.

"I hate you for how you left me," Nick said against his shoulder.

Gabriel closed his eyes. "I know."

"I really did love you."

"I know."

"That's what makes it worse."

Gabriel held him tighter but didn't say anything this time.

They stayed like that for a few seconds more—long enough for the past to come flooding back, long enough for both of them to know that whatever this had once been, it could not survive as it was.

Nick pulled back first. His eyes were red, but his voice was steady now.

"I don't want to see you again."

Gabriel stared at him, hurt washing across his face, but he nodded. "If that's what you need, I'll respect it."

"It is."

Nick backed toward the door. "And don't text me again."

Gabriel opened his mouth like he might argue, then stopped himself.

"All right," he said quietly.

Nick turned and left.

Gabriel stayed where he was, motionless in the dressing room, looking like a man who had finally gotten the truth he asked for and hated what it cost him.

When Nick came back out, Ryan could tell something had shifted immediately.

"Hey," he said gently. "You okay?"

Nick nodded, though his face was still blotchy and his eyes were glassy.

"Yeah," he said. "I think I am."

Ryan studied him for a second, then nodded back. He didn't push.

"Ready to go?"

Nick looked around the club one last time, then let out a breath that sounded lighter than the one he'd carried in.

"Yeah," he said. "I'm ready."

They didn't stay much longer. After saying their goodbyes, they stepped outside into the night air. It had been a lot—more than either of them expected—but for the first time, it felt like something had actually been put to rest.

Not neatly.

Not painlessly.

But finally.

Chapter 10
When the Truth Gets Loose

THE NEXT MORNING CAME WITH A SURPRISE—an ugly one.

It started with a single text and turned the whole day on its head before Ryan had even gotten fully out of bed. For a second, he thought he was still half asleep when his phone buzzed against the nightstand. He reached over, squinting at the screen, and saw Jim's name.

The message was short, but it hit like a punch.

Hey sorry man. Some people were asking what was going on with you, and I was still upset. I blurted it out. I'm sorry. You might be hearing from people. Sorry, man.

Ryan sat up so fast the room tilted.

His stomach dropped. His face went hot, then cold. For a moment he just stared at the message, reading it again even though he had already read enough. Then he threw the phone down onto the bed, grabbed his pillow, and shouted into it.

So that was it.

It was out.

Maybe not to everyone yet, but enough people knew now that it didn't matter. He had lost control of it. Lost control of his own timing, his own words, his own chance to tell people himself.

The first thing he thought of was his family.

Had they heard already? Had someone said something? Was he about to walk downstairs and find out his whole life had changed while he slept?

His mind raced through every possibility at once. Friends. Julie. The people from the beach. The people from the party. The ones who would be cool about it. The ones who absolutely would not. He could feel panic building fast, and under it was something just as strong—anger.

Jim knew better.

Out of everyone, he should have known better.

Ryan swung his legs off the bed and sat there for a second, trying to get a grip on himself. He needed to think. More than that, he needed someone steady.

Nick.

He got up, threw on clothes without thinking much about what he was wearing, and headed straight down the hall and downstairs to Nick's room. He knocked once, then opened the door.

Nick was already awake, sitting up in bed.

He looked surprised to see Ryan standing there so early, but the expression on Ryan's face told him immediately something was wrong.

"What's up?" Nick asked. "You look like hell."

Ryan let out a harsh breath and started pacing. "Jim texted me. He told people."

Nick frowned. "Told people what?"

"My secret," Ryan snapped. "That I'm gay. He said people were asking questions and he just blurted it out. So now I'm sitting here wondering who knows, what they've said, and whether my family is going to hear it from somebody else before I even get the chance to tell them myself."

Nick sat forward. "Fuck. That's low."

Ryan ran both hands through his hair. "I'm trying not to lose my shit, but I am seriously close. I don't even know where to start."

"Well," Nick said carefully, "if it's already moving around your friend group, then you probably need to get ahead of it where you can. Talk to the people who matter most before it gets twisted into something worse."

Ryan stopped pacing and looked at him. "I was thinking about Julie."

Nick nodded slowly. "That makes sense. She's probably one of the first people you should talk to."

"She lives, like, a block over," Ryan said. "And if she knows, then I'd rather hear what she heard straight from her. I'd rather explain it myself than let her think I hid everything from her on purpose."

Nick studied him for a second. "Are you ready for that?"

Ryan gave a hollow laugh. "No. Not even close. But I don't think that matters anymore."

Nick leaned back against the headboard. "Then just go tell the truth. That's all you can do now."

Ryan let out a long breath and sat down on the edge of the desk chair. "I'm so pissed at Jim. I trusted him. I told him because I needed to tell somebody, and he turns around and tells other people."

"Yeah," Nick said. "That sucks. When people take your truth and run with it before you're ready, it feels violating. Like they stole something from you."

"That's exactly what it feels like." Ryan looked down at the floor. "I know I can't undo it. I just want to know where I stand now. Who's actually with me. Who's not."

Nick's voice softened a little. "Then go find out. Julie first. One person at a time."

Ryan looked back up at him. "You really think I should do this alone?"

Nick nodded. "Yeah. I'll be here when you get back. But this part? I think you need to do it yourself."

Ryan sat with that for a second, then nodded once. "Yeah. You're probably right."

"I usually am," Nick said, and Ryan gave him the smallest, most reluctant laugh.

"Thanks," Ryan said. "I needed this."

"Anytime."

Ryan stood up again, calmer than when he had come in, though not by much. "All right. I'm going to get dressed, grab some coffee, and go over there."

Nick gave him a reassuring look. "You'll be okay."

"I hope so."

Ryan left the room, and Nick watched the door close behind him. Then he leaned back against the wall, smiling to himself just a little. He hated that Ryan was dealing with this, but he was glad Ryan had come to him first.

After getting dressed, Ryan went downstairs and made himself coffee. He barely tasted it. His mind was already halfway to Julie's house.

By the time he stepped outside, the day was bright and already hot. He jogged lightly down the block, then slowed to a walk as he got closer. When he reached Julie's door, he just stood there for a moment, trying to figure out what he was going to say.

Nothing sounded right.

He knocked anyway.

A few seconds later the door opened, and there she was.

Julie looked genuinely surprised to see him. Not angry exactly—just guarded.

"Hi," Ryan said. "Can we talk?"

She studied him for a second, then opened the door wider. "Sure. Come on."

They walked through the house and out onto the back patio near the pool. The sight of it hit Ryan harder than he expected. He had been there a hundred times before—for parties, late-night talks, lazy afternoons after school. He could feel all those memories pressing in while they took seats across from each other.

Julie crossed one leg over the other and looked at him directly. "So. What do you want to talk about?"

Ryan blew out a breath. "I want to talk about what you heard."

Her expression changed immediately.

"I'm guessing Jim told you," he said.

Julie nodded. "He did."

Ryan looked down briefly, then back at her. "I wanted you to hear it from me. Not from somebody else."

She didn't speak right away.

Then, finally, she said, "Are you gay?"

Ryan swallowed.

"Yes."

The word sat there between them, plain and undeniable.

Julie looked away for a second, then back at him. "Okay."

Ryan frowned slightly. "Okay?"

She let out a short breath. "Ryan, I'm not going to act like I wasn't upset. I was. At first, I was really upset. Not because you're gay—because I had to hear it from somebody else."

"That's fair."

"It felt like a betrayal," she said honestly. "We were together for a long time. We talked about everything. At least I thought we did. So yeah, hearing that from Jim instead of from you? That hurt."

Ryan nodded slowly. "I know. And I'm sorry."

Julie studied him. "Did you know?"

Ryan shook his head. "Not fully. I knew something felt off for a while, but I didn't understand what it was. Not really. I wasn't keeping it from you on purpose. I was still figuring it out myself."

Julie's face softened some. "I believe you."

Ryan looked relieved, but only a little. "I didn't want you thinking it was you."

"I know that now."

"I did care about you," he said. "I still do. Just… not in the way I thought I was supposed to."

Julie leaned back in her chair, thinking. "Honestly? That makes more sense than I expected it to."

Ryan looked up at her.

She gave a small shrug. "There were times when something felt… off. Not bad. Just off. I couldn't put my finger on it. So when I heard it, I was angry—but I wasn't shocked the way maybe I should've been."

Ryan let out a breath that almost sounded like a laugh. "That's weirdly comforting."

Julie smiled faintly. "Good."

They sat in silence for a second, and this one wasn't hostile. It was more like something settling.

"So," Julie said, "what now?"

Ryan rubbed the back of his neck. "Now, I guess I start telling people before they hear it from someone else. And at some point today… I think I need to tell my family."

Julie looked at him with something close to sympathy. "That's the one you're really scared of."

"Yeah."

"You shouldn't be."

Ryan gave her a look. "That easy, huh?"

"No," she said, "not easy. But I've known your family for years, Ryan. They adore you. You really think this is the thing that changes that?"

He looked down again. "I don't know."

"I think you do know," Julie said softly. "I think you're just scared anyway."

Ryan leaned back and stared out at the pool. "That sounds right."

Julie was quiet for a moment, then said, "For what it's worth, I'm okay. Really. I'm not thrilled that Jim got there first, but I'm okay. And I'm happy you told me yourself."

Ryan nodded. "Thank you."

She gave him a small, sad smile. "We were always better friends than anything else by the end anyway."

He looked back at her. "Yeah."

"And I still want that," she said, "the friendship."

Ryan smiled for the first time since he'd gotten the text. "Me too."

Julie stood up and walked over to him. "Come here."

Ryan stood, and they hugged. It wasn't romantic. It wasn't painful. It was just honest.

When they pulled apart, she looked him in the eye and said, "Go tell your family. Before somebody else does."

Ryan nodded. "I will."

He left Julie's house feeling lighter, though not fully calm. The conversation had gone far better than he feared. It gave him just enough courage to move on to the next thing.

He didn't want to go home immediately.

Not yet.

Instead, he headed toward the beach, putting in his headphones and starting an easy jog. The sun was brutal already, but the breeze off the water helped. As he ran, he replayed Julie's words in his mind.

You really think this is the thing that changes that?

He wanted to believe she was right.

By the time he reached the beach, it had started to fill up. People were setting up towels, music was playing in the distance, and the whole place had that bright, chaotic energy of late morning.

Ryan slowed near the shoreline, breathing hard, letting the ocean calm him.

That was when he heard someone calling his name.

He turned and saw two people waving him over from a cluster of towels and coolers and a few other people.

Zach.

Angela.

Ryan hesitated, then walked over.

"Hey," Zach said. "What's up, man?"

"Not much," Ryan said carefully. "Just out for a run."

Zach looked awkward, which was never a good sign. "So… we were just talking about you."

Ryan gave a dry smile. "I figured."

Angela looked uncomfortable, but before she could say anything, one of the other guys laughed under his breath and spoke loud enough for everyone to hear.

"So how long you been a faggot?"

The whole group went still.

Ryan felt something in him harden instantly.

Zach turned. "Dude, don't."

But the guy kept going, grinning like he thought he was hilarious. "I'm just saying, man. None of us knew. You been hiding that shit the whole time?"

Ryan stared at him. "You really want to do this right now?"

The guy shrugged. "What? Everybody's thinking it."

"No," Angela snapped. "Actually, everybody isn't."

Ryan kept his eyes on the guy. "If you've got a question, ask it like a grown man. Don't run your mouth like a twelve-year-old."

The guy stood up. "What the fuck did you say?"

Ryan didn't back up. "I said stop acting like a dumbass."

That was enough.

The guy swung first.

His fist caught Ryan in the mouth, and then both of them were in the sand, hitting, cursing, rolling while the others shouted and tried to pull them apart. Ryan got in his share of punches, but he took some too. By the time Zach and another guy managed to drag them apart, both of them were bloody and breathing hard.

"Jesus Christ!" Angela yelled. "Are you idiots done?"

Zach shoved the other guy back. "What the hell is wrong with you?"

The guy wiped blood from his lip and spat into the sand. "I'm not hanging around some fucking queer."

Ryan wiped at his mouth, tasting blood. "Then don't."

For a second, it looked like the guy might come at him again, but Zach stepped in front of him.

"Walk away," Zach said.

The guy glared at Ryan one last time, then turned and stalked off down the beach.

Silence hung over the group.

Then Angela stepped forward. "Ryan… I'm sorry."

He shook his head, still trying to catch his breath. "Not your fault."

"No, but this is exactly why people are scared to say anything," she said. "Because of assholes like that."

Ryan looked at her, surprised by how steady she sounded.

She went on, "For what it's worth, I'm glad you know who you are. And I'm sorry it came out like this."

Ryan nodded slowly. "Thanks."

Angela gave him a quick hug, then stepped back. Zach still looked miserable.

"I'm sorry too," Zach said. "I should've shut that down faster."

Ryan shook his head. "You tried."

He didn't have it in him to stay there any longer. He muttered a goodbye and jogged off before anyone could stop him.

By the time he reached home, his jaw was aching, his lip was split, and one side of his face was already starting to swell.

Great.

He stood at the front door for a second, breathing hard.

Then he went inside.

His parents, his sister, and Nick were all in the kitchen.

Every one of them turned to look at him.

The room went completely still.

Ryan stopped in the doorway, bruised, bloody, and out of excuses. He looked from one face to the next and thought:

Well. Maybe tonight came early.

Chapter 11
The Moment Before

HIS MOM HAD A WORRIED, SADDENED LOOK on her face, and for a moment no one said anything at all. The kitchen had gone strangely quiet when Ryan walked in bruised and bloodied, and even Nick, who only knew Ryan had gone to see Julie, looked stunned.

Finally, his mom spoke.

"Honey, what happened to you? Did you get into a fight? Fall? What happened?"

Ryan shifted awkwardly, already feeling the sting in his lip and cheek. "I got into it with somebody I knew down at the beach. We didn't agree on some stuff. I'm okay."

His mom immediately crossed to the freezer, grabbed an ice pack, wrapped it in a towel, and handed it to him.

"Well, I'm glad it's not worse than it looks," she said. "You'll probably have a bruise there. Just be careful, Ryan. We worry."

His dad, standing nearby, gave a small nod. "You defended yourself; I take it?"

Ryan looked over at him. "Yeah. I didn't throw the first punch."

His father nodded again, trying not to sound too approving, though Ryan could tell he respected that. "Good. Defend yourself if you need to. Just don't ever be the one to start it."

"I won't."

Nick finally spoke. "Glad you're okay, Ryan."

"Thanks," Ryan said. "I need to go clean up."

He took the ice pack upstairs with him and sat on the edge of his bed for a moment, pressing it to his face. The ache in his jaw had settled into a steady throb, and he could still hear that guy's voice from the beach, loud and ugly and full of stupid hate.

A knock came at the door.

Ryan looked up. Nick was standing there.

"Hey," he said. "Can I come in for a second?"

"Sure."

Nick stepped inside and leaned lightly against the wall. "So what happened? I knew you were going to see Julie, but I definitely wasn't expecting this."

Ryan let out a breath and lowered the ice pack. "Julie actually went fine. Better than I expected, honestly. She was upset that she heard it from someone else, but we talked it through. She wants me to be happy."

"That's good," Nick said. "So what happened after that?"

"I went for a run on the beach. Ran into some people I know. One guy started running his mouth, and I finally had enough."

Nick frowned. "Was he a good friend of yours?"

Ryan shook his head. "Not really. More like a friend of a friend. One of those guys who always says too much and thinks he's funny. Today he just pushed too far."

"What an asshole."

"Yeah," Ryan said. "That's pretty much what he is."

Nick folded his arms. "I'm sorry that happened. Some people are fine with it, and some people turn into total garbage the second they hear something they don't like."

Ryan gave a tired laugh. "Yeah, I noticed."

Nick looked at him more seriously. "I mean it, though. I'm sorry. You didn't deserve that."

Ryan nodded. "I know. I just couldn't listen to it and stand there like it was nothing."

"That makes sense."

Ryan put the ice pack back against his face. "Glad you weren't there, though. It probably would've turned into a bigger scene."

Nick made a face. "Probably. I'd want to say I'd handle it well, but honestly? I would've probably screamed at him and made it worse."

That got a real laugh out of Ryan.

"Yeah," he said. "That sounds about right."

Nick smiled. "Anyway, I'll let you get cleaned up. I just wanted to check on you."

"I appreciate it."

"Anytime."

Nick left the room and headed back downstairs. Ryan sat there a moment longer, then finally got up and went into the bathroom. He stepped into the shower and let the hot water run over him, washing away the dried blood and sweat from earlier. His mouth had stopped bleeding, but the whole side of his face still ached.

Mostly, though, he was thinking.

The fight was over.

Julie had been more understanding than he expected.

And now he was right back where he'd started—standing at the edge of something he knew he had to do.

He needed to tell his family.

The thought still made his stomach tighten. Even after everything, even after Julie's reaction and Nick's support, there was still that fear. The fear that things would change. The fear that once the words were out, nothing would ever feel the same again.

Maybe it would go fine.

Maybe they already suspected.

Maybe he was working himself up for nothing.

Or maybe he wasn't.

He stayed under the water longer than he needed to, trying to sort it all out, but no perfect plan came to him. Eventually, he shut the water off, dried himself, and changed into swim trunks.

When he went back downstairs, the family was out on the lanai. The late afternoon light hit the pool in a way that made the whole backyard look like some kind of private resort. Palm trees framed the water, and the shaded seating area looked cool and peaceful against the bright blue sky.

Ryan walked out and settled into one of the recliners in the sun.

His mom looked over at him almost immediately. "How are you feeling now?"

"I'm okay," he said. "A little sore."

"Well, if you need to talk, we're here," she said gently. "You know that."

Ryan looked at her and nodded. "I know. Thank you."

His dad was already working on dinner prep, standing by the grill and checking on what they had ready.

"I'm thinking steaks tonight," he said. "Mashed potatoes or tater tots. Maybe salad. Maybe asparagus if anyone wants it."

"That sounds amazing," Ryan said.

Nick sat up a little straighter. "I've never really had a good steak, so I'm definitely in for that."

Ryan's dad smiled. "Then tonight's your lucky night."

Ryan's mom laughed softly. "We'll make sure you're fed around here."

Nick shook his head with a smile. "You all really do a lot. I'm still not used to this."

Ryan looked over at him. "You better get used to it if you're sticking around."

Nick gave him a grateful look, but before he could answer, Ryan's dad spoke again.

"Steaks it is, then."

The mood relaxed after that. It was one of those slow, warm evenings where nobody felt rushed, where everyone kind of drifted into their own rhythm. Ryan's mom moved in and out of the kitchen, getting things ready. His dad handled the grill. His sister helped set the table outside. Nick and Ryan stayed out by the pool.

At one point, Ryan slid into the water and looked over at Nick.

"Come on in," he called. "It feels great."

Nick laughed. "All right, give me a minute."

A few minutes later, he was in the pool too, and the two of them drifted back and forth across the shallow end, talking between stretches of silence. Around them, the family moved naturally through their evening, and the more Nick watched it, the more obvious it became how much he was taking it all in.

After a while, he said quietly, "You know, I'm really enjoying this. Just… all of it."

Ryan leaned back against the side of the pool. "The pool?"

Nick smiled. "Not just the pool. All of this. You and your family. The way everyone just… is with each other."

Ryan looked over at him more closely.

Nick continued, his voice softer now. "I forgot what this looked like. People just being good to each other. No screaming. No fear. No waiting for something bad to happen."

Ryan was quiet a second before answering. "Yeah. I guess I don't always think about it because it's just what I grew up with."

"That's kind of my point," Nick said. "It's a really good thing, Ryan. I hope you know that."

Ryan nodded slowly. "I do. Maybe not all the time. But I do."

Nick smiled a little. "Good."

They stood there in the pool, shoulder-deep in warm water, while the smell of steaks drifted over from the grill.

Ryan watched his mom move between the kitchen and the patio and his dad turn the meat on the grill with practiced ease. His sister was lining up plates and silverware on the table, humming to herself. It all felt so normal. So steady.

And suddenly, for the first time that day, Ryan wondered if maybe he really didn't have anything to fear.

Maybe Julie had been right.

Maybe he was the one making it bigger than it needed to be.

Nick seemed to pick up on his shift in mood. "What are you thinking?"

Ryan let out a breath. "Just… everything."

"That helpful, huh?"

Ryan laughed. "Not even a little."

Nick moved closer to the edge of the pool. "If it helps, I still think they'll be okay. Maybe not instantly perfect, but okay."

Ryan looked at him. "You really think so?"

"I do."

Ryan was quiet for a beat. "I'm thinking maybe tomorrow."

Nick tilted his head. "Tomorrow?"

"Yeah," Ryan said. "I think maybe I tell them tomorrow."

Nick gave him a small, encouraging smile. "That sounds like a plan."

"It still scares the hell out of me."

"It should," Nick said. "That doesn't mean you shouldn't do it."

Ryan looked away toward the table, where his family was finishing dinner prep. "You make everything sound simple."

Nick laughed softly. "Oh, it's definitely not simple. You just can't wait until it stops being scary, because it won't."

Ryan shook his head, smiling despite himself. "That's not exactly comforting."

"It's honest."

"Fair enough."

They got out of the pool not long after that and dried off in the chairs while dinner was finished. Nick stretched out in one recliner, clearly relaxed in a way Ryan had never seen before, and Ryan sat beside him.

Nick looked over. "I'm excited about dinner."

Ryan laughed. "You've mentioned that."

"I'm serious. I don't think I've ever had steak like your dad's making."

"Then you're in for it. He's weirdly good at this."

Nick grinned. "I'm ready."

Ryan looked at him for a moment and smiled. "I'm glad you're here, you know."

Nick's expression softened. "Yeah?"

"Yeah," Ryan said. "I mean it. Everything's been kind of insane lately, and it helps having you here."

Nick leaned his head back against the chair. "I'm glad I'm here too."

There was something simple and real in that exchange, something that neither of them pushed any further.

A little later, Ryan went over to the grill again. "Need any help?"

His dad shook his head. "Nope. Go relax. We've got it."

Ryan smiled. "All right."

When he sat back down beside Nick, Nick asked, "No help needed?"

"Nope. Apparently, we're just supposed to enjoy ourselves."

Nick laughed. "Your mom says that every time I offer to help too."

"Yeah," Ryan said. "That's her."

"She likes taking care of people."

"She does."

"And she's good at it."

Ryan nodded. "She really is."

A few minutes later, his mom called everyone to the table.

Dinner looked incredible. Steaks, tater tots, salad, and all the extras were spread out in the middle of the table, and everyone settled in quickly. Once they started eating, the whole group went quieter in that way people do when the food is actually worth paying attention to.

Nick took one bite of steak and looked genuinely stunned.

"Oh my God," he said. "This is so good."

Ryan's dad smiled. "Glad you like it."

"I really do. This is amazing."

Ryan's mom laughed. "We're happy to feed you."

Nick looked around the table, then back at them. "I mean it, though. Thank you. For all of this. For letting me stay here. For making me feel welcome. I'm really not used to any of it."

Ryan's dad set his fork down. "You're welcome here as long as you need to be."

Nick blinked. "Really?"

"Really," his mom said. "We mean that."

His sister nodded too, like this was obvious.

Nick looked overwhelmed for a second, and Ryan could see it all over his face. "Thank you," he said again, quieter this time. "That really means a lot."

Ryan watched him for a moment and felt something shift inside himself.

Nick looked happier than he had since arriving.

Safer.

Wanted.

And sitting there, watching his family embrace him without hesitation, Ryan felt the fear inside him loosen just a little more.

Maybe this really would be okay.

Maybe this was the moment.

He looked around the table—at his parents, his sister, Nick, all of them laughing and talking and eating together—and suddenly it felt obvious. There would never be a perfect time. But if there was ever a right time, maybe it was this.

Ryan set his fork down.

His chest tightened.

Everyone was still talking when he finally said, "I have something I need to tell you guys."

The table fell quiet.

Every face turned toward him.

Ryan took a long, steady breath.

Chapter 12
The Truth at the Table

RYAN SAT THERE FOR A MOMENT, wondering if now was really the right time. Maybe it was. Maybe it wasn't. All he knew was that he needed to do it, and the sooner the better. That thought had been circling in his mind all day.

He hesitated too long.

Everyone at the table had gone quiet, waiting for him to speak, but he still hadn't said anything. He was trying too hard to figure out where to begin, when really it was simple. The question hanging over the table was obvious—what did Ryan need to say that was important enough to stop dinner for?

A minute passed. Maybe two.

Then, finally, he took another breath and spoke.

"I'm gay."

The words landed in the middle of the table and sat there. Ryan looked at each face in turn, trying to read what they were thinking before anyone said anything. Their expressions held surprise, sure, but not the kind he had feared. No one looked angry. No one looked disgusted. No one looked like they were about to turn away from him.

His mom was the first to answer. "Well, that's good," she said gently. "I'm happy for you, honey. I'm happy for you no matter what."

Ryan blinked.

His dad followed right after. "Okay. I'm happy for you too, buddy. If that's who you are, then all right."

Ryan stared at them, almost more stunned by their calm than he would have been by outrage. "Uh… thanks," he said, sounding a little lost.

His mom tilted her head. "What did you think we were going to say?"

Ryan gave a small, nervous laugh. "I don't know. I guess I expected more shock. Or pushback. I just… I wasn't expecting it to be this easy."

His mom reached across the table and laid her hand over his. "Ryan, you're our son. We love you. That doesn't change because you told us this. If anything, I'm just glad you trusted us enough to say it out loud."

His dad nodded. "Exactly. We want you happy. If this is you, then this is you. No hiding. No pretending. Just be yourself."

Ryan felt his whole body loosen at once, like he had been bracing for impact and suddenly realized it wasn't coming. "I was so nervous," he admitted. "I mean, really nervous. I've been working myself up about this for days."

"I can tell," his father said with a small smile.

Ryan let out a breath that almost turned into a laugh. "I thought there'd be more to it than this."

"Well," his mom said, smiling now too, "we could make a dramatic speech if you want, but I think 'we love you' pretty much covers it."

That got a laugh out of him, and just like that the tightness in his chest eased even more.

Nick, who had been quiet until then, looked around the table and smiled. "I'm really happy for you, Ryan. You've got a good family."

Ryan turned toward him, grateful he was there. "I'm glad you're here."

Ryan's mom looked over at Nick, her expression softening. "Was it hard for you?" she asked gently. "Coming out, I mean."

Nick's smile faded slightly. "Yeah," he said quietly. "It was hard."

The table stilled. Nick glanced down, then back up, choosing his words carefully. "My dad took it really badly. My mom too. It… wasn't anything like this."

Ryan's mom's face fell immediately. "I'm so sorry."

Nick gave a small shrug; the kind people use when they don't know what else to do with pain. "It's okay. Or, I mean, it's not okay. It just… happened."

Ryan looked at him, his own happiness now mixed with that familiar sadness he felt every time Nick talked about home. Nick seemed to notice and shook his head slightly. "This isn't about me, though. It's Ryan's moment."

"It can be about both," Ryan said quietly. "I'm okay."

Nick hesitated, then nodded.

Ryan's dad set his fork down. "What happened to you shouldn't have happened. Period. You've got a place here. You don't have to go back to something like that."

Ryan's mom nodded right away. "Again, you're welcome here for as long as you need to be."

Nick stared at them for a second, clearly overwhelmed. "Thank you," he said, his voice unsteady. "I… I don't even know what to say to that."

"You don't have to say anything," she replied. "Just know we mean it."

Ryan smiled at him. "Told you."

Nick let out a soft laugh, though his eyes looked suspiciously close to tearing up. "Yeah. You did."

"If you want to stay here, stay," Ryan's dad added, "finish school. Figure out your next step. You don't need to rush just because you're used to having the ground pulled out from under you."

Nick lowered his gaze briefly, then looked back up. "That's… a really generous offer."

"It's not charity," Ryan's mom said. "It's care."

That seemed to hit him harder than anything else. He nodded slowly. "Then I'd really like to stay. If that's okay."

"It is," Ryan's dad said. "More than okay."

Ryan could see how much that meant to him. This wasn't the usual joking, deflecting Nick—this was something deeper, something steadier.

Ryan's mom turned back to him. "And you, we are very proud of you for telling us."

Ryan smiled, still a little in disbelief. "I really thought this was going to go a lot differently."

His father shook his head. "Not in this house."

That landed in the best possible way.

The rest of the meal slowly found its rhythm again. They finished dinner, smiling more easily now, and when the plates were cleared, Ryan and Nick helped clean up. After that, everyone drifted naturally into the living room.

No one made the moment bigger than it needed to be. That was maybe the best part. No interrogation, no drawn-out tension—just acceptance, plain and simple. They picked a movie, settled in, and let the evening continue.

By the time it ended, Ryan's parents and sister headed off to bed, leaving him and Nick alone in the living room with the TV playing softly in the background.

For a while, neither of them spoke. The quiet wasn't awkward—it was comfortable. Ryan glanced over at Nick a few times before finally turning toward him.

"Hey… when you came out, your dad just hit you?"

The question came out more bluntly than he intended, but Nick didn't seem offended. He just went still for a moment.

"Yeah," he said quietly. "He did."

Ryan swallowed. "What about your mom?"

Nick's expression changed immediately. He dropped his gaze, his breathing shifting—subtle at first, then faster. His hands began to shake slightly.

"Nick?"

No answer.

Ryan leaned forward, his voice steady. "Hey, you're okay. Breathe. Look at me."

Nick struggled for air, panic creeping in. Ryan stayed calm, grounding him. "In… and out. You're here. You're safe."

It took a minute, maybe two, but slowly Nick's breathing steadied. The panic loosened its grip.

They sat in silence for a moment after that.

"My mom…" Nick started, then stopped, swallowing hard. "She didn't always stop him. Sometimes she screamed. Sometimes she cried. Sometimes she just… checked out. When she was high, it was worse. Not because she hit me—but because she wasn't there."

Ryan didn't interrupt.

"That was the part that messed me up the most," Nick continued quietly. "At least with my dad, I knew what I was dealing with. With her… I kept hoping she'd choose me. And sometimes she tried. But not when it mattered most."

Ryan's chest tightened. "You deserved better."

Nick finally looked at him. "Yeah," he said softly. "I know that now."

Ryan nodded. "And you've got better now."

Nick's expression eased just a little. "Yeah. I think maybe I do."

They sat there a while longer, the TV playing to a room that was no longer watching it. The night had become heavier than expected, but not in a bad way.

It felt honest.

And for the first time in a long time, both of them were in a place where honesty didn't come with consequences.

Chapter 13
What He Couldn't Forget

NICK SAT THERE FOR A MOMENT, trying to steady his breathing. The panic had passed, but everything he had pushed down for years was still sitting just beneath the surface. He ran a hand over his face, trying to compose himself enough to speak, but the memories were already there—sharp, vivid, and impossible to ignore.

Ryan didn't rush him. He had no idea what to say after what he had just witnessed, and for once, he didn't try to fill the silence. Instead, he stayed where he was, giving Nick the space to recover, knowing that whatever came next had to come on Nick's terms.

After a moment, Ryan spoke carefully. "How are you feeling? I'm sorry if I asked something I shouldn't have. I didn't mean to push."

Nick shook his head slowly. "No… it's not that. I'm okay. It just brings back things I've tried to forget for a long time. I wish I could, but I can't."

"You don't have to say anything you don't want to," Ryan said gently, watching him. "Really."

Nick didn't respond right away. His gaze dropped to his hands, but his mind was somewhere else entirely—back in that moment, replaying everything with a clarity he hated.

"She was high," he finally said, his voice low. "I don't know on what or how much. She came into my room late that night… barely dressed. I remember that part clearly."

He paused, jaw tightening as the memory pushed forward.

"She covered my mouth and kept saying, 'No son of mine is a faggot.' Over and over. She hit me—slapped me across the face—and just kept going. Saying things… calling me disgusting, a disgrace."

Ryan stayed still, listening without interruption.

"It didn't stop there," Nick continued, his voice unsteady. "Something changed. She got more aggressive, angrier. I couldn't really fight back—I was already dizzy from being hit. Everything felt off, like I wasn't fully there."

He swallowed hard, his hands clenching together.

"I wanted to stop her. I wanted to push her away… do something. But I couldn't. I just froze. Completely."

Tears slipped down his face as he shook his head. "I couldn't move. I couldn't think. It was like my body just shut down."

He let out a shaky breath, struggling to keep going. "She crossed a line no one ever should. And I didn't know what to do. I just… wasn't there anymore."

That was as far as he could go.

Ryan didn't ask for more. He didn't need to. He moved closer and wrapped his arms around Nick, pulling him into a steady, grounding hug. Nick leaned into him and broke, crying hard—the kind of crying that comes from years of holding something in.

Ryan didn't speak right away. He just held him there, letting him get it out.

After a while, when Nick's breathing began to slow, Ryan spoke softly. "None of that was your fault. Not any of it. Freezing like that—that's not weakness. That's what happens when something overwhelming hits you all at once."

Nick shook his head slightly. "I should've done something."

"You did," Ryan said gently. "You survived it. That matters."

Nick let out a breath that almost sounded like a laugh, but there was no humor in it. "I just felt so… useless. Like I couldn't even defend myself."

"That's not how it works," Ryan replied. "You didn't choose that moment. It happened to you, and your body reacted the only way it could."

Nick didn't argue this time. He leaned back slightly, wiping his face, still trying to settle himself.

"I used to think about getting out all the time," he admitted after a moment. "Running away. Never going back. But somehow, I always ended up there again."

Ryan nodded. "That makes sense. Leaving isn't always as easy as it sounds."

Nick gave a tired smile. "Yeah. But I'm out now. And I'm here. That's what matters."

"It does," Ryan said. "And you're safe here. You don't have to go through anything like that again."

Nick looked at him, something softer in his expression now. "I know. And I'm really grateful for that. For you… for your family. This place—it's different. In a good way."

Ryan smiled. "I'm glad we're here for you."

Nick nodded. "It helped… telling someone. I've never said that out loud before. Not to anyone."

"I'm really glad you told me," Ryan said. "Seriously. I don't know exactly what that feels like, but I'm here for you. Whatever you need."

Nick let out a slow breath. "Thank you. That means a lot."

They sat there quietly for a few minutes, letting everything settle into something more manageable.

Eventually, Ryan stretched and glanced toward the stairs. "I didn't realize how late it got. I think I'm gonna head up."

"Yeah," Nick said. "Me too."

Ryan stood, then paused. "Hey… thanks for trusting me with that."

Nick gave a small, genuine smile. "Thanks for listening."

Ryan nodded and headed upstairs, leaving Nick alone in the quiet.

Nick sat there a while longer, thinking about everything—about what he had just said out loud for the first time, about how it felt to finally not carry it alone. It didn't fix anything, but it felt lighter somehow.

Still, he knew that was only part of it. There was more—things he wasn't ready to say yet.

Eventually, he got up, grabbed a glass of water from the kitchen, and headed upstairs. Outside, the night was clear and still, the stars bright overhead. For the first time in a long time, it felt like something new was beginning.

The rest of the night faded into quiet. After everything that had been said, neither of them had much left to give, and sleep came easier than expected.

The next day passed without much conversation about it. There was an unspoken understanding between them—Nick had shared something heavy, and Ryan didn't need to push. Just being there was enough.

By the following night, things felt steadier. Not perfect, not resolved—but steadier. Enough to breathe. Enough to move forward.

In his room, Nick stood in front of the mirror, focusing on something simple—what to wear, how to look, something he could control. He picked out a tan button-down shirt and a pair of shorter blue shorts, casual but sharp. He added a few rings, then slipped on his beaded bracelet, the blue and white worn smooth from years of use.

After running mousse through his hair and styling it into a messy, intentional look, he stepped back and checked himself.

"Damn," he muttered with a smirk. "I look good."

Upstairs, Ryan was getting ready too. A fitted blue polo and black shorts—clean, simple, effortless. He adjusted his hair in the mirror, giving it just enough structure, then stepped back and smiled.

Tonight felt different.

He headed downstairs and waited by the door, a mix of nerves and excitement settling in. When he heard movement upstairs, he looked up just as Nick appeared, coming down the stairs.

Ryan grinned immediately. "Look at you. You clean up really well."

Nick laughed. "You're not doing too bad yourself."

Ryan nodded toward the bracelet. "That's cool, by the way."

Nick glanced down at it. "Yeah. A friend made it for me."

Ryan smiled. "He did a good job."

Nick looked back up. "You ready?"

Ryan grabbed his keys. "Yeah. Let's go."

Together, they stepped out into the night.

Chapter 14
Learning to Breathe

NICK LAY IN BED unable to sleep, his mind circling everything that had happened. He was glad he had told Ryan some of the truth about his past, but there was still so much more beneath it. What he shared about his mother was only one piece of a much larger, darker history. There was a long list of things he had endured, and an equally long list of things he had done just to survive. Ryan only knew the surface of it, and Nick wasn't sure how much more he could bring himself to say.

The fact that he had told anyone anything at all was a huge step. In a strange way, he felt lighter—less alone. But at the same time, the more he thought about it, the more he realized that telling the truth would only get heavier from here. He had never imagined he could say any of it out loud, yet now that the first barrier had broken, everything else seemed to be pressing forward, waiting.

What would happen to their friendship once everything was out? Would Ryan still look at him the same way? Would things change? Nick didn't know. Part of him was terrified, while another part just wanted to keep going—wanted to unload everything that had been buried for so long. He had carried so much anger and pain that he didn't even know what to do with it anymore. Still, maybe if someone truly understood, something good could come from it.

Across the house, Ryan wasn't sleeping much better. He tossed and turned, unable to stop replaying the conversation from the night before. It felt unreal—like something out of a nightmare—but it wasn't. That was what kept hitting him. How could something like that happen to someone? How could anyone do that?

He had a thousand questions, but he knew better than to ask too many. It was clearly one of the worst parts of Nick's life, and pushing too hard could make things worse. Still, he couldn't help but feel there was more to the story. He was almost certain of it.

By the time night gave way to morning, neither of them had truly slept. The sun slowly rose, casting light across the sky. It should have felt peaceful, but both of them knew the day ahead carried weight. Maybe that wasn't a bad thing. Maybe something good could come from finally facing everything.

Nick eventually gave up on sleep. He got up, splashed water on his face, and stared at himself in the mirror for a moment, trying to steady himself. Then he threw on a robe, grabbed a drink from the fridge, and stepped out onto the lanai. It was quiet, calm, and empty. The pool shimmered in the early light, and for a moment, he just sat there, letting himself breathe.

A faint sound behind him broke the silence.

He turned and saw Ryan stepping outside.

"Guess you couldn't sleep either?" Nick asked.

Ryan shook his head. "Not really. I kept thinking about what you told me."

Nick sighed. "Yeah… same here. It just brought everything back."

Ryan leaned forward slightly. "I'm sorry. I just… I can't even imagine going through something like that. It's hard to wrap my head around."

Nick nodded. "I wouldn't wish it on anyone. I just hope it gets easier over time. I try to push it away, but it's always there."

Ryan paused, then said, "It may always be there, but it doesn't define you. You're more than what happened to you. You made it out—that matters. You're here now."

Nick gave a small, tired smile. "Yeah… I guess that's true. And talking about it actually helped. More than I thought it would."

"I'm glad," Ryan said. "And I appreciate you trusting me. That couldn't have been easy."

Nick looked at him. "It wasn't. But something about you… it just felt safe to talk."

Ryan hesitated for a moment, then spoke carefully. "I feel like there's more you want to say. You don't have to—but if you want to, I'm here."

Nick exhaled slowly. "There is more. A lot more."

He leaned back slightly, gathering his thoughts.

"It really started getting worse when I was around eleven. My dad was deep into alcohol and drugs, and he got my mom into it too. After that, everything just spiraled."

Ryan frowned. "That must've destroyed any sense of normal life."

"It did. The only place I ever felt somewhat normal was at the club. That became my escape. It was the only place I could actually be myself."

Ryan nodded. "That makes sense. You found somewhere you could breathe."

Nick let out a quiet laugh. "Exactly. Anywhere but home."

He paused, then continued.

"I thought about leaving for good a lot, but I never had the courage. As messed up as it sounds, I still felt tied to them… especially my mom."

Ryan nodded slowly. "That kind of connection is hard to break, even when it hurts."

Nick looked at him again. "Yeah… it is."

He took a breath, then added quietly, "If I'm going to tell you more… you might want coffee for this part."

Ryan gave a small nod. "Yeah… probably."

They went into the kitchen. The house was still quiet, the rest of the family asleep. Ryan started the coffee while Nick grabbed mugs and creamer. When it finished, they took their drinks back outside and sat in silence for a moment before continuing.

Nick stared out toward the pool, his grip tightening slightly around his coffee cup.

"When I was about eleven, my parents started sending me to a dealer's house to pick drugs up for them," he said. "At first, it was once a week… then more often. They didn't want to go themselves anymore."

Ryan frowned but stayed quiet.

"The guy… he wasn't right," Nick continued hesitatingly. "He was a perv," he finally blurted. "He'd say things. Try to push boundaries. Tell me he wanted to take pictures of me in my underwear, and I could keep the money my parents had sent me with. He offered different ways I could 'pay' too."

Nick shuddered, as the memory washed over him. "I never went along with it. I told him, 'Fuck no!' grabbed what I came for and got out. But every time I went there, it felt like I was walking into something I couldn't control."

He stopped, jaw tightening. "Yeah, he was a fucking pervert. Into kids. Sick piece of shit.

"And it didn't stop there. At home, things were just as bad—worse, sometimes. All my parents cared about was getting high, and all I was good for was being their drug runner. As long as they had what they needed, it didn't matter what I needed. And if I didn't do what they wanted, things escalated. Fast. So I learned to do whatever it took to keep things from getting worse."

Ryan's expression shifted, more serious now.

Nick took a breath before continuing, his voice quieter.

"There were times I had to make choices no one should ever have to make. Things I didn't want to do. Things I still hate thinking about. But back then… it felt like survival. Like there wasn't another option."

Silence settled heavily between them for a moment.

"When they didn't have money, they had me sell drugs to get their next fix. Sometimes I stole stuff. Sometimes they had me do 'favors…'" Nick trailed off.

"Favors?" Ryan asked, afraid he already knew the severity of that single word.

"Yeah, if they didn't have money, they pimped me out. I was 16 when I first did it. Just a kid. These guys didn't care. They just wanted payment for their drugs. You have no idea how fucking bad it was."

"I felt like I didn't belong to myself," Nick added a steely edge taking over his tone. "Like I was just something they used when they needed to. I mean, when you don't even have any control of your own body..." he trailed off, his gaze focused on something from the past.

"And no matter what I did, it was never enough. They could do whatever they wanted to me at any moment. And if I even thought about putting up any resistance, I'd get the shit beat out of me.

"I just wish they could get a taste of the shithole life they put me through. See what it's like to ruin someone's life and use and abuse someone you're supposed to love and be caring for.

"Seriously, I've thought about killing them." It came up almost as a whisper. "I mean, I wouldn't actually, but I've thought about how much my life would be better without them in it."

Ryan swallowed hard, anger flickering across his face, but he kept his voice steady.

"That's not on you," he said. "None of that is on you."

Nick didn't respond right away. He just nodded slightly, eyes still fixed ahead.

"I know that now," he said after a moment. "At least... I'm starting to."

Nick sat quietly after speaking, his emotions still close to the surface. He looked out toward the pool, jaw clenched, trying to steady himself.

Ryan sat there, stunned and angry all at once. It was hard to process everything he was hearing. He felt sick thinking about it, but more than anything, he felt for Nick.

"That's... a lot," Ryan said finally, choosing his words carefully. "No one should ever have to go through anything like that. I get why you'd feel angry. I really do."

Nick nodded, his voice quieter now. "I just wanted out. That's all I ever wanted."

"And now you are," Ryan said. "That's what matters. You're here now. You're safe."

Nick looked at him, something softer in his expression. "Yeah... and for the first time in a long time, I actually feel like I belong somewhere. I feel like I can breathe."

Ryan smiled slightly. "I'm glad."

They sat there for a while longer, letting the weight of everything settle. Eventually, Nick spoke again, more calmly.

"I just want to focus on what's ahead now. I want to make something of my life. I don't ever want to become anything like them."

"And you won't," Ryan said. "You already proved that."

Nick nodded. "I just need to stay focused. That's all."

"You will," Ryan said, "and you don't have to do it alone."

Nick gave a small smile. "I know. And that means more than you probably realize."

Ryan leaned back in his chair. "Same here. Honestly, I didn't expect things with my family to go as well as they did either. I thought it would be a whole thing. But it wasn't."

"Not everyone gets that," Nick said.

"No," Ryan agreed. "But I'm grateful I did."

They both sat quietly for a moment, then exchanged a small, genuine smile.

For the first time, things didn't feel quite as heavy.

As the morning continued, the rest of the family began to wake up and joined them outside. Coffee turned into a light breakfast, and conversation flowed easily. No one else knew what had been said earlier, but Nick and Ryan shared occasional glances, both aware that something had shifted between them.

The day had only just begun.

And neither of them knew where it might lead.

Chapter 15
The Weight of What We Did

RYAN MOVED INTO THE KITCHEN and began cleaning up from the morning, rinsing dishes and stacking them neatly in the rack. He always liked to help out when he could; it gave him something steady to focus on, especially after everything Nick had shared earlier. The quiet rhythm of it helped settle his mind, but it didn't stop the memories from surfacing.

As he scrubbed a plate, a flashback hit him—middle school, the beginning of when everything started to shift. Back then, he was already a standout: strong in sports, sharp in class, and well-liked by just about everyone. By seventh grade, he had built a reputation as someone untouchable—a jock, confident, admired. Most people didn't mess with him, and his circle of friends, mostly from football and baseball, made sure of that.

Still, he never let that define him entirely. He tried to balance everything—the athlete, the student, the friend. Girls gravitated toward him, and people expected him to follow a certain path. But there had been one friend who didn't quite fit into that mold, someone different in a way Ryan couldn't quite name at the time. They had grown close, often hanging out away from the larger group. It had felt easy, natural—until it didn't.

There had always been something Ryan couldn't fully understand about him. A certain closeness, moments that felt just slightly off. At the time, Ryan hadn't wanted to examine it too closely. Looking back now, he wondered if that curiosity—those small questions he ignored—

had been part of something deeper in himself, something he wasn't ready to face.

Nick stepped into the kitchen with a couple of dishes, pulling Ryan out of his thoughts. He set them down and grabbed a water before the two of them headed out to the lanai. The house was quiet; everyone else was busy with their own routines. It left the space open, calm—just the two of them again.

Ryan leaned back in his chair, exhaling slowly. "We talked a lot about your past," he said, glancing over. "There's something I've never really told anyone. I think… it's part of why I've always felt different. It goes back to middle school, but I didn't handle it well."

Nick's interest sparked immediately. "Okay. Now I'm curious."

Ryan nodded, taking a moment before continuing. "I was deep into sports by then—football, baseball—the whole thing. I had a lot of friends, but this one guy and I spent a lot of time together, just the two of us. He was… different. Not in a bad way. Just not like everyone else. And sometimes, he got a little too close. I didn't know what to make of it back then."

He paused, choosing his words more carefully now. "One day we were hanging out here, actually—swimming, messing around, nothing serious. Eventually we went inside to play video games, and I jumped in the shower. I didn't think anything of it, but at some point, I realized he was standing there, watching. Not just casually—really watching. It caught me off guard."

Nick's expression shifted, more focused now. "And you didn't know how to handle it."

"Not even close," Ryan admitted. "I reacted badly. I got angry, grabbed him by the throat, told him, 'Stop looking at me. I'm not gay.'

"He kept apologizing. I told him he'd pay if people found out he was gay. I panicked. I didn't want anyone questioning me, didn't want anything about me to change. I thought I had everything figured out, and suddenly I didn't."

His voice lowered. "And then I made it worse. I told someone. Just one person. But you know how that goes. It spread. Fast."

Nick didn't interrupt.

"Some of the guys went after him," Ryan continued. "Cornered him, beat him up. I was there. I didn't stop it... I even joined in. I kicked him in the stomach." Ryan shook his head in dismay, sick from his own actions. "No one said anything afterward. No one had to. It just... happened."

Ryan stared out at the pool. "He started getting bullied in school pretty bad. People were always saying shit about him, making fun of him. I just laughed along with them.

"Not long after that, he was gone. His parents pulled him out of school before the year ended.

"He was beaten up and bullied all because of me. I made him the joke of the school. And I did absolutely nothing to stop it. Worse, I was part of the problem." Nick could hear the anger and disgust in himself, in Ryan's voice.

"Inside, I felt awful, because, you know, he was one of my best friends. I didn't know what to do though, so I went to his house once, tried to see him. His mom answered. They were packing up and moving. She told me to leave and not come back."

"I'm not sure if she knew it was me or not that started the whole thing," Ryan continued, "but I just didn't want anyone to think I was gay, you know? I had to get away from it somehow. But I didn't mean to hurt him. That sounds dumb, now, but I didn't think of the consequences for him. I definitely didn't want him to have to move away."

Nick sat with that for a moment before responding. "I can definitely understand him leaving. He was probably scared for his life, being bullied and beaten up. Not saying it wouldn't happen elsewhere, but, yeah, if I had a chance to leave a situation like that, I'd want to leave too. Then, on top of it, he lost your friendship."

"That kind of thing... it escalates fast, especially at that age," Nick sighed. "Fear, pressure, trying to protect how people see you—it makes people react without thinking. It made you react. Doesn't make it right. It's definitely not an excuse, but I've seen it happen."

Ryan nodded, though his expression stayed heavy. "I didn't think about it like that then. I just wanted distance from it—distance from him, from what it meant. But I've thought about it a lot since. I didn't just walk away; I helped push him out. That's on me. All because I didn't want anyone to think I was gay. Kind of ironic now, huh?" Ryan concluded with a mirthless chuckle.

Nick leaned forward slightly. "The difference now is that you see it. You understand it. That matters more than you think. People grow. You were kids dealing with something neither of you knew how to handle."

Ryan let out a slow breath. "I've thought about trying to find him. Apologize. I don't know if it would change anything, but maybe it would be something."

"It might," Nick said, "or it might not. But if it gives you some peace, it's worth trying. Not everything gets fixed, but sometimes just owning it is enough."

Ryan nodded. "Yeah. I think so too."

They sat quietly for a moment, both processing their own pasts in the shared silence. Neither story was easy, and neither had clean endings—but there was something grounding in being able to say it out loud.

Nick finally spoke again, softer now. "For what it's worth, I don't think you're that person anymore."

Ryan glanced over. "I hope not."

"You're not," Nick said simply.

The weight between them shifted—not gone, but lighter. The kind of understanding that didn't need to be explained further.

Time passed without either of them noticing. The sun had climbed higher, and the quiet morning had turned into early afternoon. They had been sitting there, talking, unpacking pieces of themselves without even realizing how much time had slipped by.

There was something different about it—something steady. No judgment, no pressure. Just two people learning how to trust each other with the parts they didn't usually share.

And somewhere beneath all of it, unspoken but present, was a quiet question neither of them had quite figured out yet:

Was this just friendship—or the beginning of something more?

Chapter 16
The Connection

RYAN HAD DONE A LOT OF THINKING over the last few days, so much that his mind felt worn out. But no matter where his thoughts started, they always seemed to circle back to Nick. It was strange, really. In the middle of everything changing in his life, Nick had somehow become the one steady thing keeping him grounded. Every time Ryan thought about him, he found himself smiling without even realizing it.

He kept thinking about that too brief kiss from before, about the feeling that had been there between them, even then. The more time they spent together, the harder it was to ignore the possibility that something real was developing. He just didn't know if Nick still felt that way.

Nick, meanwhile, had gone out to lie by the pool and soak up the sun. It was hot already, the kind of heat that settled into your skin and made it easy to stay still. He stretched out on the lounger and let himself relax, though his mind was anything but quiet. He had been thinking about Ryan a lot too—about how easy it had become to talk to him, to trust him, to want to be around him. He was starting to admit to himself that what he felt wasn't just friendship.

That realization scared him a little.

He had never imagined himself falling for someone like Ryan. Not because Ryan wasn't attractive—he obviously was—but because he seemed like the kind of guy who would always have one foot somewhere else. Ryan had a future waiting for him, a whole life opening up in another city. He would be leaving for school, starting something new, moving ahead. So what could possibly come of whatever this was?

Still, Nick couldn't stop thinking about the possibility. He didn't want to rush anything, especially with Ryan being so new to all of this, but the curiosity was there. Maybe there really was something between them. Maybe it would be worth finding out.

Ryan eventually came out to the pool too and stretched out in a nearby chair, not saying anything at first. The two of them just lay there in the heat, listening to the faint sounds of the neighborhood and the water moving lightly in the pool. It was the kind of afternoon meant for doing nothing at all.

But even in the quiet, both of them were thinking the same thing.

Ryan knew there was something different happening between them. It wasn't only that they had become good friends in such a short amount of time. It was deeper than that—built on things they had told each other, trusted each other with, things they had never said out loud before. That kind of honesty meant something. He could feel it.

Nick was trying not to overthink things, though that was nearly impossible. Every now and then, he glanced over at Ryan and wondered what it would actually be like if they tried this—whatever "this" was. He already loved Ryan's family and felt more at home there than he ever had in his own house. In some ways, the idea of becoming something more with Ryan felt natural. In other ways, it felt risky. What if it made everything complicated?

The problem was, ignoring it wasn't getting any easier.

After a while, Nick broke the silence. "You know, your family has been so good to me. I still don't think I've really wrapped my head around it. Letting me stay here, wanting me to finish senior year here... that's huge. I never thought I'd actually have a real shot at a future. Not like this."

Ryan turned his head toward him and smiled. "I'm glad they've made you feel that way. If they said you can stay, they meant it. They really do want that for you. And honestly, I've liked having you here too. A lot."

Nick smiled back, softer this time. "I've liked it too. It feels like I have something real for the first time in a long time. Not just a place to crash or people to hang around with. Something solid. I know I keep saying it, but I really am glad we met."

"I am too," Ryan said. "I don't think I would've handled any of this as well without you around. You made me feel like I wasn't alone in it. Like I could actually be myself and not freak out about it. I still can't believe you knew before I fully admitted it to myself, but I guess part of me always knew too."

Nick gave a small shrug. "Well, now you've admitted it. And you're still here. Still yourself. Just more honest."

Ryan let out a breath and looked over at him again, holding his gaze a little longer this time. "Yeah," he said quietly. "I think I am."

Something shifted in the silence that followed. Neither of them looked away right away, and the air between them seemed to change—subtle, but real. It wasn't hard to see anymore that they were both feeling it.

Ryan was the first to speak.

"You know," he said carefully, "I've been thinking a lot about that kiss the other night. Or… almost-kiss, I guess. And I keep wondering what it meant to you."

Nick looked at him, a little thrown off. "Honestly? I didn't really think it through. I just felt something and went for it. After, I was like… yeah, maybe I totally read that wrong."

Ryan shook his head. "Nah. It just caught me off guard, that's all. I wasn't ready for it right then. But… I've been thinking about it."

Nick glanced over. "Yeah?"

Ryan shrugged, casual but not really. "Yeah. Feels like there's something there. I just don't know what yet."

Nick let that sit for a second. "I've thought about it too. I didn't know if it was just everything going on or… something else."

Ryan nodded slightly. "Same. It just doesn't feel like only a friend thing anymore though."

A beat passed.

"Yeah, I get that." Nick laughed under his breath, nervous but pleased. "So what are you saying, Ryan?"

“I’m saying maybe we shouldn’t ignore it,” Ryan said. “Maybe we should see where it goes.”

Nick blinked at him, clearly surprised, “You mean… actually try this? Like, really see if there’s something here?”

“Yeah.”

Nick sat with that for a moment, then smiled slowly. “I’d like that.”

Ryan smiled too, and just like that, some of the tension between them eased. It was still new. Still uncertain. But now it had a shape to it.

Nick shifted in his chair. “So what happens now? Do we go on an actual date or something?”

Ryan laughed softly. “I mean… yeah, I guess that’s exactly what we do.”

“A real date?” Nick asked, grinning now.

“A real date,” Ryan confirmed. “Dinner, at least. Maybe more, if we feel like it. Nothing too big. Just… us.”

“Yeah, I’d be into that,” Nick said. “I just don’t wanna make it weird or anything. We can just… see what it is.”

Ryan nodded. “Yeah. Same. I don’t really know what I’m doing here, but I’m down to try.”

Nick’s expression softened. “That’s enough.”

Ryan could feel both nerves and excitement building at once, but somehow it didn’t feel terrifying. Not the way he might have expected. It felt new, sure, but also right. That was the part he couldn’t ignore.

They sat there for a while longer, both smiling now, the kind of quiet settling over them that comes after something important has finally been said.

After a bit, Nick got up and headed into the kitchen for something to drink. He came back out with a glass in his hand and sat down again, looking out at the pool before glancing over at Ryan. Even just watching him sit there in the sunlight made something twist pleasantly in his chest. Ryan was gorgeous, sure, but it wasn’t only that. He was kind. He listened. He cared. That was what kept pulling Nick toward him.

A moment later, Ryan’s mom stepped outside with her keys in hand.

"Hey, Ryan—we're going to be out tonight," she said. "There's money on the counter if you boys want to get food or go do something. Have fun."

"Okay," Ryan called back. "Have fun too. See you later."

Nick smiled. "Have fun."

Once the door closed behind her, Ryan looked back at Nick. "Well… I guess that makes tonight easier."

Nick laughed. "Yeah, I guess it does."

"I know a really good Mexican place not too far from here," Ryan said. "We could go there for dinner. And if you want, maybe we hit the club afterward."

"That sounds perfect," Nick said. "I'm not even going to pretend I'm not excited. Because I really am."

Ryan grinned. "Me too."

The reality of it hit them both then: this was happening. Their first real date. Ryan's first date with a guy at all. The thought made him nervous, but in a way that felt alive instead of frightening.

He ended up slipping into the pool a little while later, floating on his back and letting the cool water balance the heat of the day. After a minute, he heard movement and looked over to see Nick joining him.

"You decided to get in too?" Ryan asked.

"Yeah," Nick said, dipping under the water before resurfacing. "You looked way too relaxed over here. I wanted in on that."

Ryan laughed. "It is pretty great."

Nick floated nearby, letting the water hold him up. "I think that's one of the biggest differences here," he said after a moment. "I can relax. I don't have to be waiting for something bad to happen. I don't have to keep one eye open all the time."

Ryan's expression softened. "I'm glad. You deserve that."

Nick looked over at him. "I know. I'm starting to believe that."

They drifted there for a while, talking on and off, the conversation moving easily between them. Every so often they caught each other looking and smiled without meaning to. The connection between them had only grown stronger now that they had finally said what had been hanging in the air all day.

As the afternoon wore on, the date ahead loomed larger in both of their minds. For Nick, it felt exciting and familiar in some ways, though this was different than anything he'd had before. For Ryan, it was something entirely new—a first in every sense that mattered. That alone made it meaningful.

And yet neither of them wanted to rush past what it was.

This was the beginning of something. Maybe not something permanent, not yet, but something real enough to be worth finding out.

Could two people really get this close this fast?

Maybe.

Or maybe some connections simply arrive already feeling familiar, as if they had been waiting for the right moment to happen.

Either way, by the time the sun began to dip and the evening started inching closer, both Ryan and Nick knew one thing for certain:

They were looking forward to what came next.

Chapter 17
The First Date

THE DAY SLIPPED AWAY as evening settled in, the sky softening toward sunset. The house was quiet, just Ryan and Nick. They climbed out of the pool and dried off, the air still warm against their skin. Ryan dropped into a chair, catching his breath, while Nick paused on his way inside, already thinking ahead.

"I'm gonna go get cleaned up and figure out what I'm wearing," Nick said, glancing back. "Might take me a bit."

Ryan nodded, still relaxed. "Yeah, I'll be in soon. Just gonna sit here for a minute. Should be a good night though. I'm looking forward to it."

Nick smirked lightly. "Same. Don't take too long."

Ryan watched him disappear inside, then leaned back, letting the quiet settle around him. His mind kept drifting back to Nick—how easy things had felt lately, how different everything was. It wasn't just the night ahead. It was everything building underneath it. After a minute, he stood, grabbed a drink from the fridge, and headed upstairs to shower.

Up in his room, Nick stood in front of the mirror, cycling through outfits, tossing shirts aside until something finally clicked. Looking good mattered to him—it always had—but tonight felt different. This wasn't about attention or being seen. This was about Ryan noticing.

He adjusted the collar, turned slightly, checked himself again. "Yeah… that works," he muttered, a small, satisfied smile pulling at his lips.

In the next room, Ryan had already changed twice before settling on something simple but sharp. He looked at himself in the mirror, exhaled slowly, and gave a small nod. It felt right—nothing overdone, just enough.

When he got downstairs, he hovered by the door and called up, "Nick, you ready?"

"Yeah—coming down."

A second later, Nick appeared at the top of the stairs, and Ryan's eyes locked onto him without meaning to. He didn't even try to hide it.

"Damn," Ryan said quietly. "You look… really good."

Nick caught the tone more than the words and smiled, a little slower this time. "Thanks. You clean up pretty well too."

Ryan huffed a quiet laugh, rubbing the back of his neck. "Yeah, well… figured I should at least try."

There was a brief pause, something unspoken sitting between them, before Ryan grabbed his keys and nodded toward the door. "You ready?"

"Yeah," Nick said, holding his gaze a second longer than necessary. "Let's go."

The restaurant wasn't far—modern, warm, just upscale enough to feel like it mattered. Ryan parked, and they walked in side-by-side, close enough that their shoulders brushed once or twice without either of them moving away.

They were seated quickly, and a waitress came over with an easy smile. "Hi, I'm Maria. What can I get you started with?"

"Coke," Nick said.

"Same," Ryan added. "And queso."

Once she left, they both glanced at each other, a small, almost amused silence settling in.

Ryan leaned back slightly. "So… what do you think?"

Nick looked around, taking it in. "It's nice. Didn't expect this."

"Yeah, I like it. Food's good too."

Their drinks came, then the chips, and for a few minutes they didn't say much—just ate, letting the nerves burn off. By the time the waitress came back, they ordered easily, slipping into something more natural.

Nick rested his arm on the table, watching Ryan. "You've been quiet. What's going on in your head?"

Ryan shrugged, but there was a small smile there. "Nothing bad. Just… I don't know. I'm glad we're doing this."

Nick's expression softened a little. "Yeah. Me too."

Ryan held his gaze for a second longer than usual. "Feels easy. Being around you."

Nick let out a quiet breath, almost like he hadn't realized he'd been holding it. "Yeah… it does."

Dinner passed in that same rhythm—comfortable, steady, with moments where they'd catch each other looking and not immediately look away. By the time they stepped outside again, the air had cooled just enough to make the night feel wide open.

They started walking, and after a few steps, Nick reached for Ryan's hand.

There was a brief hesitation—just long enough to matter—but then Ryan's fingers closed around his. It wasn't perfect or smooth. It felt new. But he didn't let go.

Nick noticed.

Neither of them said anything.

The club was already alive when they walked in—music pulsing, bodies moving, the energy immediate and loud. It wrapped around them as soon as they stepped inside.

"Near the bar, Raul spotted them and grinned, lifting his drink in greeting. Ryan recognized him right away from the last time they'd been there—the guy who seemed to know everyone, effortlessly working the room like it was his own.

"Hey! There you are!" Raul called out, waving them over. "We were wondering when you'd come back."

Nick smirked as they approached, clearly more at home here. "Took a minute, but we made it."

Raul pulled Nick into a quick one-armed hug, then clapped Ryan on the shoulder like they were already on familiar terms. "Good. We missed you."

Ryan smiled, a little more relaxed now. "Yeah, figured we'd stop by."

Raul's eyes flicked between them for just a second—quick, observant—but he didn't say anything about it, just gave a knowing grin.

"Drinks?" he asked, already turning toward the bar.

Drinks came fast. Shots followed. The night picked up speed before Ryan could overthink any of it.

Nick was in his element—already moving, already pulled into the music. Ryan stayed back at first, leaning against the table, watching him. Watching how easily he fit into all of this. Watching how good he looked doing it.

"Come on!" Nick called over the music, reaching for him.

Ryan shook his head, smiling. "I'm good right here."

That lasted thirty seconds.

Nick came back, grabbed his wrist, and pulled him in anyway. This time, Ryan didn't fight it.

At first, he was stiff—unsure where to put his hands, how to move—but the music was loud enough to drown that out. Slowly, he loosened, falling into the rhythm. Nick stayed close, guiding him without making it obvious, their bodies brushing more often than necessary.

It wasn't just dancing anymore.

At one point, Ryan's hand landed on Nick's waist—and stayed there. Nick didn't react, didn't pull away. If anything, he leaned into it just slightly, like he wanted to see if Ryan would notice.

He did.

And he didn't move his hands.

Later, they stepped outside with a couple of Raul's friends, the night air cooler now, the street still alive with music and traffic. Someone suggested ice cream, and nobody argued. It felt like the kind of random late-night plan that only happened when everyone was in a good mood.

Ryan walked beside Nick while the others moved ahead, laughing too loudly about something neither of them were listening to.

Nick bumped Ryan lightly with his shoulder. "You survived the dance floor."

"Barely."

"You were getting into it."

"I was adapting."

Nick laughed. "That hand on my waist looked pretty adapted."

Ryan glanced at him. "You complaining?"

Nick's grin widened. "Not even a little."

That look stayed between them all the way to the shop.

They got cones and took over two outside tables, still riding the buzz of the night. Ryan felt lighter than he had in weeks. Nick was animated, talking with Raul and the others, then turning back to Ryan every few seconds like some part of his attention kept returning there automatically.

Ryan noticed.

He liked noticing.

Nick leaned toward him while Raul argued dramatically about toppings.

"You having a good time?"

Ryan looked at him. "Yeah."

"Just yeah?"

Ryan smirked. "Better than yeah."

Nick held his gaze a beat too long, then smiled to himself.

That was when Gabriel appeared. He was hand-in-hand with someone neither Nick nor Ryan recognized. They slowed like someone had given them an invitation.

The tension hit immediately, sharp and uncomfortable.

"Well, look who it is," Gabriel sneered,

The whole group shifted.

Nick's expression hardened immediately. "Gabriel."

Gabriel's eyes slid to Ryan, taking his time.

"And this must be the replacement."

Ryan said nothing.

Gabriel gave a fake thoughtful look. "I'm sorry. What was your name again." I smirk marred his features. "Oh, right. Virgin."

Nick stood before Ryan could answer.

"You know his name."

Gabriel shrugged. "Do I?"

"You do," Nick said sharply. "So cut the shit."

The street noise around them suddenly felt far away.

Gabriel smirked, but it wavered for a second. "Relax. I'm just surprised. Didn't think you'd move on this fast."

Nick stepped closer. "You left. Remember that part?"

Ryan rose slowly too, calm but solid.

"Why don't you keep walking," Ryan said. "You've got somebody with you. Focus on that."

Gabriel turned to him fully now.

"Oh, he talks."

Ryan didn't move.

Gabriel looked him over once, then laughed under his breath.

"You have no idea what you signed up for."

Nick's jaw flexed. "Enough."

"No, seriously," Gabriel said, eyes still on Ryan. "He does this in the beginning. Makes you feel special. Needs all your attention. Wants every second. Then suddenly you can't breathe without him taking it personally."

Raul pushed back from the table. "Man, nobody asked for the TED Talk."

A couple of the others laughed, but the tension stayed sharp.

Gabriel ignored them.

"He'll act easygoing now," he said to Ryan. "Give it a week."

Ryan took one step forward.

"You done?"

Gabriel's smile thinned. "Touchy."

"No," Ryan said evenly. "Just bored."

That got a louder laugh from the group.

Gabriel's date shifted awkwardly beside him. "Can we go?"

Gabriel didn't look at him.

Ryan's voice dropped lower.

"You came over here because you wanted a reaction. Here it is: nobody cares. So walk away."

For a moment, it looked like Gabriel might say something worse. Instead, he gave Nick one last bitter glance, before turning back to Ryan.

"You'll figure it out." Gabriel said as he turned and walked off, dragging his embarrassed companion with him. "You'll see. He's a leech and will be so stuck to you, you won't be able to shake him," Gabriel threw that last comment over his shoulder, and stalked away.

Nobody spoke for a second.

Then Raul clapped once.

"Well. That killed the vibe."

The group slowly restarted around them, conversations returning in pieces, but Ryan's focus stayed on Nick.

Nick stared down the sidewalk where Gabriel had disappeared.

Ryan stepped closer. "Hey."

Nick looked at him.

"Don't let him get in your head."

Nick exhaled slowly. "I'm trying not to."

Ryan held his eyes. "He came over because he saw you happy."

That landed.

Nick's expression shifted, tension easing just slightly.

"You think so?"

"I know so."

Nick studied him for a second, then gave a small smile.

"You always this good at reading people?"

"No," Ryan said. "Just assholes."

Nick laughed—real this time.

The weight of the moment cracked.

Raul pointed his spoon at them. "Great. Emotional breakthrough achieved. Can we get back to ice cream now?"

Everyone laughed, including Nick.

He sat back down beside Ryan, this time closer than before, their knees touching under the table and neither moving away.

As the group talked around them, Nick leaned in quietly.

"Thanks."

Ryan glanced at him. "For what?"

"For not making that weird."

Ryan held his gaze. "Tonight's been too good to let him ruin it."

Nick looked at him for a long second, something warm and unguarded passing across his face.

"Yeah," he said softly. "It has."

When they finally headed back to the car later, the others peeling off in different directions, the night felt quieter again.

Ryan reached for Nick's hand first this time.

Nick looked down at it, then up at him, smiling.

"Well, look at that," he said.

"Shut up."

Nick laced their fingers together. "Best part of the night," he said.

Ryan didn't answer.

He just held on tighter.

Back at the house, everything was dark. They moved quietly through the kitchen, grabbing water, neither of them rushing to end the night just yet. At the top of the stairs, they split, and Nick entered his room, closing his door softly behind him. Ryan continued down the hall towards his room, then stopped and turned back.

He stood outside Nick's door, heart pounding harder than he expected. For a second, he almost walked away.

Then the door opened.

Nick blinked, surprised. "Hey… you good?"

Ryan didn't answer right away. He just stepped inside.

The door closed behind them, and the air shifted—thicker, quieter.

Ryan moved first.

He reached for Nick, pulled him in, and kissed him—this time without hesitation.

Nick froze for half a second, caught off guard, then kissed him back just as hard. There was nothing unsure about it now. No testing. No pulling back.

Ryan broke first, breathing a little uneven. "I've been thinking about that all night."

Nick's lips curved slightly, still close. "Yeah?"

Ryan nodded, voice low. "Yeah."

That was all it took.

Nick kissed him again, slower this time, deeper. His hand slid up along Ryan's jaw, holding him there, like he didn't want him to pull away again. Ryan's hands found his waist, pulling him closer until there wasn't space left between them.

Everything felt sharper—heat, breath, the way their bodies lined up without trying.

Ryan hesitated for just a second, something flickering in his head—

—but Nick felt it and pulled him back in before he could overthink it.

"Hey," he murmured, just barely pulling back. "You good?"

Ryan met his eyes, searching for a second… then nodded. "Yeah."

That was enough.

They didn't rush it after that. It wasn't frantic—it was deliberate, like both of them were learning the moment as it happened. Hands moved slower, more certain. The tension built instead of breaking.

Time stretched without either of them noticing.

By the time the first hint of morning started to creep in through the window, neither of them had said much. They didn't need to.

Something had shifted.

Not just curiosity anymore.

Something real.

And neither of them was pretending they didn't feel it.

Chapter 18
Close, But Not There

THE SUN PUSHED THROUGH THE WINDOW in thin, bright lines, already warming the room. Outside, it looked like another perfect day—clear sky, heat rising early—but inside, everything felt just slightly off.

Ryan woke first.

For a second, he didn't move. He just stared at the ceiling, replaying pieces of the night—flashes, not everything, but enough. The way things shifted. The way it didn't feel like just a normal night anymore.

That was the problem.

It *wasn't* just a normal night.

Before Nick stirred, Ryan quietly got up and slipped out of the room, easing the door shut behind him. The second he was in the hallway, he exhaled like he'd been holding it in.

He wasn't panicked. He wasn't regretful.

But he wasn't settled either.

Back in his own room, he dropped onto his bed and ran a hand over his face, trying to organize his thoughts. He felt good about what happened—he really did—but now that it was morning, everything felt… different. Like there was something unspoken sitting between them already.

And he didn't know what to do with that yet.

Nick woke a little later, reaching out instinctively before realizing the space beside him was empty.

For a moment, he just lay there, blinking at the ceiling, trying to piece things together through the haze. Then it hit him all at once—everything from the night before—and a slow smile pulled at his mouth.

It hadn't been nothing.

That much was clear.

But right behind that came something else—hesitation. Not regret, but awareness. Things had shifted, whether they said it out loud or not.

He sat up, rubbing the back of his neck, the dull edge of a hangover creeping in. After a second, he pushed himself out of bed and headed to the bathroom, bracing his hands on the sink as he looked at himself in the mirror.

"Don't make it weird," he muttered under his breath.

Simple enough in theory.

By the time Nick came downstairs, Ryan was already in the kitchen, pouring coffee. He glanced up when Nick walked in, just for a second, then grabbed another mug and filled it without saying anything. Small, normal. Easy.

Nick noticed.

"Thanks," he said, grabbing the creamer and following Ryan out to the lanai.

They settled into the loungers like they had every other morning—same seats, same view, same routine. Only now, everything felt just a notch more careful.

Nick took a sip of his coffee, then broke the silence first.

"Last night was good."

Ryan nodded once. "Yeah. It was."

A beat passed.

Nick shifted slightly, looking over at him. "I mean… all of it. Not just going out."

Ryan let out a small breath through his nose, staring out toward the yard for a second before answering.

"It wasn't bad," he said. "Just… different."

"Different good?" Nick asked.

Ryan hesitated, then shrugged. "Yeah. Just—" he paused, searching for the right words, "I don't want it to screw things up between us."

Nick nodded slowly. "Yeah. Same."

That part, at least, was easy to agree on.

Ryan leaned forward slightly, resting his forearms on his knees. "I think I just need to slow it down a bit," he said. "Figure my own shit out first. I don't want to jump into something and mess it up."

Nick held his gaze for a second, then nodded again, more firmly this time.

"I get that," he said. "We're good where we are. No reason to rush anything."

It was the right answer.

Even if it wasn't the one he would've picked.

They let the conversation drop after that, both of them easing back into something more familiar—finishing their coffee, moving around the kitchen, talking about nothing in particular.

Eventually, Ryan glanced over at him. "We should get out of here today. Do something."

Nick didn't hesitate. "Beach?"

Ryan smirked slightly. "Yeah. That works."

The beach was already warm by the time they got there, the air thick with heat but cut by a steady breeze off the water. It felt normal again—sun, sand, noise—something they could both sink into without overthinking.

For a while, they kept to themselves. Headphones in, stretched out in the sun, not saying much. It helped.

Until it didn't.

"Yo—Ryan!"

The shout cut through everything.

Ryan pulled one earbud out, already knowing the voice before he turned his head.

Zach.

Of course.

A few yards away, Julie was with him, along with a couple of the others. They had set up close enough to be a problem, not close enough to pretend it was an accident. Ryan kept his face neutral, though his jaw had already gone tight. Beside him, Nick lowered his sunglasses and followed his line of sight without saying anything.

"Just ignore it," Nick muttered.

Ryan gave the smallest nod, but Zach was already coming over.

He walked up with that same cocky half-smile Ryan had seen a hundred times before, the one that usually meant he was about to say something stupid and expect everybody else to laugh.

"Damn," Zach said, looking between Ryan and Nick. "So it's really like that now?"

Ryan stayed seated a second longer, forcing calm into his voice. "Morning to you too."

Zach laughed under his breath. "Come on, man. Don't get touchy. I'm just saying—you disappear for a few days, come back acting different, and now you're out here playing house on the beach."

Nick shifted beside him, but Ryan lifted a hand slightly without taking his eyes off Zach.

"We're good over here," Ryan said. "So why don't you head back to your people?"

Zach tilted his head, pretending to consider it. "Nah. Think I'll stay a minute." His eyes slid to Nick. "You two serious, or is he just experimenting?"

Ryan stood then, slow and deliberate.

"That's enough."

Something in his tone made Zach straighten, but the smirk stayed.

"What?" Zach said. "You don't want people asking questions now? Bit late for privacy, isn't it?"

Ryan stepped closer. "Walk away."

Zach gave a short laugh. "Look at you giving orders. Since when? You couldn't even be honest with Julie, and now you're acting hard because you found yourself a beach boyfriend?"

Nick rose now too. "Back off, Zach."

Zach barely glanced at him. "I'm talking to him."

Ryan's jaw flexed. "Then talk carefully."

For a second, the air between them felt razor-thin.

Then Zach leaned in, voice lower, meaner.

"You really threw everything away for this? Your friends. Your reputation. All of it… including Julie."

That hit harder than Ryan expected.

Not because it was true.

Because Zach said it like he'd been waiting to.

Ryan's voice dropped. "You don't get to talk about Julie."

"Why not?" Zach shot back. "You clearly weren't that into her. Everybody knew something was off with you."

Ryan stepped closer, chest nearly touching his.

"Say one more word."

Instead of looking worried, Zach smiled. "Maybe she figured it out before you did."

That was the line.

Ryan shoved him hard in the chest, sending him backward into the sand.

Zach came up swinging wild. Ryan slipped the first punch and landed one clean across Zach's mouth. Zach lunged again, tackling him low, and they crashed into the sand hard enough to draw shouts from half the beach.

They rolled, grappling, sand flying. Zach got a fistful of Ryan's shirt. Ryan drove an elbow free and hit him again. Years of resentment came with it—every cheap comment, every public dig, every time Zach needed an audience. Zach needed to be taught a lesson, and Ryan was going to be the one who gave it to him.

"Ryan!" Nick shouted, grabbing for his shoulder.

Two other guys rushed in from Zach's side, pulling at arms and dragging them apart.

By the time they were separated, both of them were breathing hard. Zach had blood at the corner of his mouth now, sand stuck to his face, rage replacing every trace of swagger.

"You lost your damn mind?" he snapped.

Ryan wiped his lip with the back of his hand. "No. You just finally pushed too far."

Zach jerked against the guys holding him. "This isn't over."

Ryan took a step forward despite Nick's hand on his arm. "Then next time finish what you start."

Julie had reached them by then.

"Zach," she said sharply, "drop it. Now."

He looked at her, then back at Ryan, still burning.

"This is why everybody gets tired of your shit," he muttered.

Ryan didn't blink. "Then stay tired somewhere else."

Zach spat blood into the sand, yanked free, and backed away.

As he turned, he threw one last look over his shoulder. "You always ruin everything around you."

Then he walked off.

Julie lingered.

For a second, neither she nor Ryan said anything. The old familiarity of her being there pressed in harder than he wanted it to.

Finally she said, quieter now, "I didn't know he was going to do that."

Ryan let out a breath and looked toward the water. "Yeah. Well. He did."

She nodded, uncomfortable. "I'm sorry."

He studied her for a second, then gave a tight nod. "It's fine."

It wasn't. But it also wasn't hers to carry.

She gave him one last look, then headed back toward the others.

Ryan watched her go for half a second before Nick handed him a towel.

Ryan took it, breathing hard, adrenaline still running hot.

"Come on," he said at last. "Let's grab something to eat."

Nick looked at him a moment, then nodded. "Yeah. I could eat."

The burger place was just off the beach, where they had been. It was a small, crowded spot, the kind of place everyone knew about but never stayed in long. The smell of grilled meat and salt air hit them before they even stepped inside.

Ryan slowed just slightly as they approached the counter.

Nick noticed.

"You good?" he asked, low.

Ryan nodded once. "Yeah. Just… haven't been here in a minute."

That wasn't the whole truth, but Nick let it go.

They stepped up to the counter, and Ryan scanned the menu like he hadn't already decided what he wanted. It took him a second to look up.

Then he froze.

Behind the register stood Jim.

For a beat, neither of them said anything.

Jim leaned back slightly, like he'd just realized who he was looking at, and let out a short breath through his nose.

"Well," he said. "Look who decided to show up."

Ryan gave a small, tight smile. "Hey, man."

It wasn't hostile.

But it wasn't easy either.

Nick glanced between them, picking up on it immediately—the kind of tension that doesn't need explaining.

Jim's eyes flicked to Nick, then back to Ryan. "You been avoiding this place, or just me?"

Ryan shrugged, casual on the surface. "Little bit of both."

Jim gave a quiet huff, not quite a laugh. "Yeah. That tracks."

Another pause settled in, heavier this time.

Ryan broke it first. "You still working here full-time?"

"Yeah," Jim said. "For now." Then, after a beat, "Saw you out there earlier."

Ryan nodded. "Yeah."

"Zach's still an idiot," Jim added flatly.

That got the smallest real reaction out of Ryan—a quick half-smirk. "Hasn't changed."

Jim studied him for a second longer than necessary. "You haven't either," he said.

Ryan didn't respond to that.

Nick shifted his weight slightly, letting them have it but staying close enough to feel the edges of the conversation. There was history here—real history—not just casual friendship.

Jim tapped the counter lightly. "You ordering, or just standing there making it awkward?"

Ryan exhaled through his nose. "Yeah. I'll take a double cheeseburger, fries, and a Coke."

Nick ordered after him, keeping it simple.

Jim rang it up, movements efficient, but his eyes kept drifting back to Ryan like there was something he wanted to say and hadn't decided how.

As Ryan handed over the cash, Jim said, quieter now, "You around for a little bit?"

Ryan hesitated, just for a second. "Maybe."

Jim gave a small nod. "I have a break in a few minutes."

Ryan glanced toward the door, then back at him. "We'll be outside."

"Yeah," Jim said. "Figured."

They grabbed their drinks and found a small table outside, tucked just far enough from the crowd to feel like their own space.

Nick sat across from him, watching.

"That your best friend?" he asked.

Ryan nodded once. "Yeah. Or… was."

He didn't elaborate, and for once, Nick didn't push. Whatever was there, it wasn't surface-level.

Their food came out a few minutes later, and they ate mostly in silence, the noise of the beach carrying over the low hum between them.

Halfway through, Jim stepped out from the side door, wiping his hands on a towel before tossing it over his shoulder. He spotted them immediately and walked over, pulling out a chair without asking.

"Got a few minutes," he said.

Ryan nodded. "Cool."

Jim leaned back, looking between the two of them again before settling on Ryan. "So."

Ryan didn't ease into it.

"You and Zach been hanging out a lot?" he asked.

Jim shrugged. "Here and there."

Ryan let that sit for a second. "You know about him and Julie?"

Jim gave him a look. "Yeah. I know."

"Since when?"

Jim hesitated, then leaned forward slightly, lowering his voice.

"They've been circling each other for a while," he said. "Way before you guys actually ended it."

Ryan's jaw tightened, just barely. "How long is 'a while'?"

Jim shook his head. "I don't know exact timing. But it wasn't new this summer."

That landed.

Nick stayed quiet, but he saw it—the shift in Ryan's face, subtle but real.

Jim kept going. "Honestly, man… things between you and her were off way before that anyway."

Ryan looked down at the table. "Yeah. I know."

Jim studied him for a second, then added, "It was after that summer, though. That's when everything changed."

Ryan's head came up slightly.

"What do you mean?" he asked.

Jim frowned, thinking. "I don't know. You came back different. Quieter, I guess. Not in a bad way. Just… not the same. And she picked up on it. Everybody did."

Ryan didn't say anything.

Jim leaned back again. "Whatever happened that summer—" he shrugged lightly, "—that's when things shifted."

Silence settled over the table.

Nick didn't look at Ryan right away. He didn't need to. He could feel it.

That one sentence had hit something.

Jim pushed his chair back after a second. "I should get back before I get yelled at."

He stood, glancing between them. "Good seeing you, man."

Ryan nodded. "Yeah. You too."

Jim looked like he might say something else, then thought better of it and headed back inside.

As Jim re-entered the burger joint, Nick asked, "You good?"

"Yeah," Ryan replied. But his voice said he wasn't.

Nick studied him for a second. "That didn't feel like nothing."

Ryan huffed out a quiet laugh. "It wasn't."

A pause.

Then Nick added, a little more carefully, "Julie still gets to you."

Ryan didn't answer right away.

"Not like that," he said eventually. "Just… history."

Nick nodded. He understood that.

Some things didn't disappear clean.

Ryan sat there meticulously folding the wrapper his burger had been in, carefully reinforcing each crease. Nick watched each careful fold, hoping somehow the inward folding of the wrapper would lead to the outward unfolding of Ryan.

"I didn't tell you everything about that summer," Ryan said without looking up from the now square of foil.

Nick looked up, immediately focused. "Yeah?"

Ryan nodded, jaw tightening slightly.

"I think that's when things really started changing," he said. "And I know why now."

He finally looked at Nick.

"I just never told anyone."

Chapter 19
The Summer That Changed Everything

RYAN SAT THERE FOR A LONG MOMENT, staring down at the folded wrapper like it might tell him where to start. It wasn't just a story—it was something he had buried so deeply that even thinking about it made his chest tighten. Now that it was pushing its way back up, he wasn't sure how much of it he was ready to say out loud.

Across from him, Nick didn't rush him. He leaned back in his chair, iced coffee in hand, watching without pressing. Ryan had already learned that about him—Nick knew when to talk and when to just let things come.

Ryan exhaled slowly and rubbed his hands together once. "Okay," he said. "So… last summer…"

He paused, then tried again.

"My family took a trip to Maine. Mount Desert Island for part of it. It was actually great—quiet, clean, just… different from here. I started running in the mornings while we were there, just to get out and clear my head. That's where I met him."

Nick stayed quiet, letting him continue.

"His name was Alex," Ryan said. "He ran the same trails. We ended up talking one morning, then running together the next. It was easy at first. Normal. Just two guys running, talking shit, comparing routes, joking around. Nothing strange about it. I didn't think much of it."

Ryan's jaw tightened.

"Honestly… I liked talking to him. He was easy to be around. Confident. Funny. He knew the trails, showed me places I never would've found on my own. I remember thinking he was cool."

Nick said nothing.

"Then one morning we ran up this trail to an overlook. No one else around. Just trees, water, and the two of us. We were both catching our breath. I thought it was just another run."

Ryan stared past Nick now, seeing the past all over again.

"He stepped closer and started talking different. More personal. Asked if I had a girlfriend. Asked if I'd ever fooled around with anyone while traveling. Stuff like that."

Nick's eyes narrowed slightly.

"I laughed it off. Tried to make it nothing. Then he smiled like he already knew something I didn't."

Ryan swallowed.

"He said I gave off a vibe."

Nick stayed quiet.

"I asked him what the hell that meant. He said, 'You know exactly what I mean.' Then he touched me."

Ryan's hand clenched on the table.

"Not by accident. Not joking around. He put his hand on me like he'd already decided who I was."

He shook his head sharply at the unwanted memory.

"And that's what set me off."

Ryan's voice hardened.

"It wasn't just that he touched me. It was that he thought he had me figured out. Like he could look at me and label me. Like he knew something about me before I did."

Nick watched him carefully but stayed silent.

"I felt embarrassed. Exposed. Pissed off. And if I'm being honest…" Ryan paused. "Probably scared too."

He exhaled hard.

"Because part of me reacted to it before my brain did. I hated that."

That hung there.

"So I snapped."

Ryan looked down at his hands.

"I hit him. Hard. He stumbled, and I hit him again. Then again. And again. I don't even know how long it went on. It was like something just took over and I couldn't shut it off. I wasn't thinking—I just needed it to stop. After that it wasn't even about him anymore. It was everything at once—anger, confusion, panic. I just kept going."

He paused, swallowing. "When I finally backed off, he was down. Barely moving. That's when it hit me what I'd done."

Ryan rubbed at his jaw.

"I panicked. Hit the emergency button on his watch. Then I ran."

Nick watched him carefully. "So you weren't just mad at him."

Ryan gave a short, bitter laugh. "No. I was mad at him. But I was madder at what it brought up in me."

Nick watched him carefully. "Did anything happen after that?"

Ryan shook his head. "That's the thing—nothing. No police. No one asking questions. No one at the hotel. Nothing. I never even found out if he was okay."

Nick nodded slowly. "You called for help. That matters."

Ryan let out a quiet breath. "Yeah. Maybe."

He then leaned back and ran a hand slowly over his face. "That should've been enough to mess with me. But it wasn't just guilt. It was the fact that I couldn't stop thinking about why I got that mad in the first place. And there was more."

Nick's focus sharpened. "Okay."

Ryan hesitated longer this time.

"This happened later that same week," he said. "Different day. I stopped at a coffee place one morning. Some guy outside asked me to spot him for a drink. Seemed normal enough, so I did. Thought nothing of it."

He paused, then continued more quietly.

"He followed me inside. Caught me off guard. And I didn't react the same way I did with Alex. I didn't swing. I didn't fight. I just... froze."

The word hung there.

"It was over fast," Ryan said. "And then he acted like it was nothing. Like we had some kind of understanding. Then he just left."

Ryan stared at the table.

"I stood there trying to process what had just happened. Told myself it didn't matter. That I could ignore it and move on. But something about that week stuck with me whether I wanted it to or not."

He leaned back slightly.

"I came back different. Didn't want to admit it, but things weren't the same. That's when everything with Julie started falling apart. I didn't feel the same anymore. Couldn't explain it at the time, but I knew something was off—and she did too."

Nick nodded. "So that's when you knew."

Ryan gave a faint shrug. "I think part of me knew. I just didn't want to deal with it. Not then."

They sat quietly for a moment, the café noise fading into the background.

Finally Nick spoke. "So when people push at you, corner you, or cross a line… that's what it hits."

Ryan exhaled. "Yeah. I don't like feeling out of control. Both of those situations did that, just in different ways."

Nick leaned back, thinking. "You didn't handle either of those perfectly," he said. "But that doesn't make you some villain either."

Ryan gave a humorless half-smile. "Doesn't exactly feel great."

"No," Nick said. "But it also doesn't mean everything's on you."

Ryan nodded slightly. "I've had that sitting in my head for over a year. Never told anybody."

"Well," Nick said, steady, "you told somebody now."

Ryan looked at him, and something in his expression eased—just a little.

"Yeah," he said quietly. "I did."

They sat there a moment longer before Ryan straightened up.

"We should probably get out of here."

Nick stood. "Yeah. Let's walk."

They left the café and wandered without much direction, just following the sidewalk until the noise of the lunch crowd faded behind them. Neither of them spoke for a while. Nick recognized the difference now. This wasn't comfortable silence. Ryan was still turning things over in his head.

Eventually, they stopped into a small clothing shop, more out of instinct than intention. The place had a mix of vintage and newer pieces, everything with a slightly different edge to it.

Nick immediately started browsing, flipping through racks, clearly more at home in a place like this. Ryan followed, not really looking for anything, just trying to reset.

At one rack, Nick pulled out a shirt—blue with white accents, a little flashier than anything Ryan would normally wear.

"You should try this," Nick said, holding it up with a grin.

Ryan looked at it skeptically. "That's not me."

"Just try it," Nick said. "You might surprise yourself."

Ryan shook his head but took it anyway. A few minutes later, he stepped out of the fitting room wearing it, clearly unsure.

Nick took one look and started laughing. "Okay… I'm not gonna lie—that's not your usual look. But it works more than you think."

Ryan looked down at himself, then back up. "You serious?"

"A little," Nick said, still smiling. "Not saying it's everyday you, but it's not terrible either."

Ryan snorted and shook his head, heading back to change. "Yeah, no. That's staying here."

They both laughed, the tension easing a bit.

Nick ended up picking out a few things for himself—nothing over the top, just enough to refresh what he had. Ryan, meanwhile, wandered a bit more aimlessly until something small caught his eye—a simple bracelet with an "N" etched into it.

He picked it up, turning it over in his hand for a second, then added it to what he was holding without saying anything.

When they finished, they paid and stepped back out into the street.

They wandered a little longer, stopping in a couple more places, but Ryan's focus kept slipping. Something was still pulling at him—something from that same summer he hadn't fully said yet.

Nick noticed.

"You've been off since that first store," he said finally. "You sure you're good?"

Ryan blinked, like he'd been pulled out of something. "Yeah. Just… thinking."

Nick studied him for a second but didn't push further. "All right."

They made their way back to the car, bags in hand, and headed home.

By the time they pulled into the driveway, the house was already busy again. Ryan's mom was unloading groceries, calling out to them as they got out.

"Hey! Perfect timing. You two mind helping?"

They jumped in, carrying bags inside and putting things away. It was normal, easy—exactly what Ryan needed to level himself out.

Afterward, he grabbed a drink and headed out to the pool. The sun was still high, the water calm, everything quiet again.

Nick joined him a few minutes later.

"You just needed a reset, huh?" Nick said, dropping into a chair.

Ryan gave a small nod. "Yeah. Something like that."

They sat in the sun for a while before Ryan got up and slid into the pool, letting the water close over his head.

Nick watched him for a moment, then spoke more carefully.

"You know… earlier—at that first stop—you checked out for a minute. That wasn't just random."

Ryan surfaced, brushing water back from his face.

"It wasn't," he admitted.

Nick nodded. "You don't have to say anything. Just… if you want to, I'm here."

Ryan leaned back against the edge of the pool, thinking.

"It was that same coffee place," he said finally. "The one I told you about. I hadn't thought about it in a long time, and then it just… came back."

Nick didn't move. "You want to talk about it?"

Ryan took a breath.

"Yeah," he said. "I think I do."

Nick leaned forward slightly. "All right. Go ahead."

Ryan nodded once, steadying himself.

"I'll tell you what really happened."

Chapter 20
What We Carry

RYAN STAYED IN THE POOL a moment longer, his arms resting along the edge while he tried to decide how much he really wanted to say. Water ran from his hair down his face and shoulders, but he barely noticed. Nick waited nearby in the lounge chair, not pushing, just giving him room. The sun was still high and hot over the patio, and for a while the only sounds between them were the quiet splash of water and the muffled movement of the house behind them.

Finally Ryan spoke.

"Well… something did happen to me," he said quietly. "And I didn't know what to make of it then. I'm still not sure I do."

Nick turned toward him a little more fully. "All right."

Ryan let out a slow breath. "It was at that coffee shop I told you about. There was this guy outside asking for coffee money. He didn't look homeless or anything, just like he was down on cash and needed a break. I bought him one. Thought I was just doing something decent. Then I went inside to use the restroom. The place was quiet, hardly anybody around, and before I could come out of the bathroom, he came in after me."

Nick sat up straighter, but he didn't say anything.

"He grabbed me and pulled me into a stall. Had me pinned before I even understood what was happening." Ryan stared out across the yard. "He forced himself on me. Went down on me before I could process any of it. That's the part that's always bothered me most. I froze. I just froze."

The words sat there between them.

"When it was over, he walked out like nothing happened. Like it had all been normal. Like I'd agreed to it." Ryan's jaw tightened. "I fixed myself up, stood there for a minute trying to breathe, then went back out front. He was already gone."

Nick stayed quiet for a few seconds before he said, "That wasn't your fault."

Ryan gave a short, humorless laugh. "Didn't feel that way."

"I mean it," Nick said. "Freezing doesn't mean you wanted it. It means you were shocked."

Ryan looked over at him then, like he hadn't expected that answer to come so fast or so firmly. "I spent a long time telling myself I should've fought harder."

"You shouldn't have had to fight at all."

That hit Ryan harder than he wanted to admit. He looked away again and dragged a hand over the back of his neck.

"There's more," he said after a moment. "That's the part that really messed me up."

Nick nodded once. "Then tell me."

Ryan pushed off the wall and stood in the shallow end, pacing once through the water before turning back. "About a week later, I was out running early. The beach was mostly empty, still dark enough where everything looked half-asleep. I saw somebody sitting alone near the shoreline, but I didn't think much of it until he spoke."

He swallowed.

"It was him."

Nick's expression hardened. "The same guy?"

Ryan nodded. "He recognized me right away. Started talking like we had some kind of history. Like what happened at the coffee shop was mutual." His voice sharpened at that. "I told him to stay the hell away from me. Told him what he did was wrong."

"And?"

"He came closer anyway. Said I didn't stop him the first time. Said deep down I wanted it."

Nick muttered, "Piece of shit."

Ryan gave a grim little nod. "I told him to back off. He didn't. Then he kissed me."

Nick went still, but didn't interrupt.

"I shoved him," Ryan said. "But for a second…" He shook his head. "For a second, I kissed him back. Then I hit him."

Nick didn't move, didn't react beyond the look in his eyes.

"I hit him hard. A couple times. He dropped, and after that I backed off." Ryan's face twisted with disgust, mostly at himself. "I kept thinking, why did I kiss him back? Why did I hit him after? Why did any of it happen like that?"

Nick answered carefully. "Because you were angry. Because you were confused. Because he crossed a line and then tried to make you feel like it was your choice."

Ryan rubbed both hands down his face. "Maybe."

He lowered them slowly and looked out toward the fence. "Then I looked up and saw somebody standing farther down the beach."

Nick already knew that part mattered. "Who?"

Ryan met his eyes. "Julie."

Nick blinked once. "She saw?"

"I don't know how much she saw. Enough." Ryan climbed out of the pool and sat on the edge, water dripping onto the concrete below him. "I didn't put it together until now. Why she came back different after that summer. Why senior year felt off almost from the first day."

He stared past Nick, seeing another version of himself entirely. "First week of school she pulled me aside and said something like, let's just get through the year. Said we were both leaving after graduation anyway, so we should keep things simple and make it through. At the time I thought she was just being weird, or distant, or maybe mad at me over something stupid. But now…" He let out a slow breath. "Now I think she knew something had changed in me before I did."

"She might have," Nick said softly.

Ryan nodded. "I think she saw enough to know I wasn't who she thought I was. Maybe she didn't know exactly what it meant. Hell, neither did I."

They sat with that for a while. The quiet between them wasn't awkward, just heavy.

Then Nick said, "You've been carrying that whole thing by yourself."

"Yeah."

"No wonder it keeps coming back."

Ryan looked over at him. "I didn't realize how much of my life changed because of one summer."

Nick held his gaze. "Maybe it wasn't just one summer. Maybe it was the first time you couldn't lie to yourself anymore."

Ryan let that settle. He didn't answer, but he didn't argue with it either.

The mood shifted slowly after that. Ryan swam a few lazy laps just to move, while Nick stayed stretched out in the chair, watching sunlight flicker across the water and trying to give Ryan the space to come back to himself. After a while Ryan climbed out again and dropped into the lounge beside him, damp and quieter than before.

"What are you thinking?" Ryan asked.

Nick smirked faintly. "Honestly?"

"Dangerous start."

"I'm thinking you've lived about five lives already."

That got a real laugh out of Ryan. "Yeah, well. Some of them weren't great."

Nick turned his head toward him. "You're still here though."

Ryan glanced back at him. "Barely knew you a week ago and now you know more about me than anybody."

"That bother you?"

Ryan actually thought about it. "No," he said after a moment. "Actually, no."

Nick smiled at that, and for a few minutes they just listened to the sounds coming from inside the house—cabinet doors, footsteps, Ryan's mom moving around in the kitchen. Normal life. Safe life.

Then Nick's expression changed a little. "I was thinking about my mom earlier."

Ryan turned toward him immediately. "Yeah?"

Nick nodded, staring up at the sky instead of at him. "She could be awful. Most days she was checked out, high, angry, or just gone in every way except physically. But sometimes she wasn't. Sometimes she'd have ten minutes where she sounded like somebody else. Ask if I ate. Ask how school was. Tell me I should get out of there one day."

Ryan stayed quiet and let him keep going.

"Then she'd disappear again," Nick said. "That's what messes with me. I hate what that house was, but I still think about whether she's okay."

"That makes sense."

"Does it?"

"Yeah," Ryan said. "People can hurt you and still matter to you. Both can be true."

Nick turned that over and then gave a small nod. "I don't want to go back there."

"Then don't."

Nick looked at him.

"I mean it," Ryan said. "Stay here as long as you need. Figure out what comes next when you're ready."

Something softened in Nick's face at that. "You and your family really mean that, don't you?"

"We do."

Nick looked away fast, like he didn't want to be caught reacting too much. "I'm not used to that."

"I know."

The afternoon stretched warm and slow around them after that. Nick eventually pushed himself upright and looked over at Ryan again.

"You know what that club was for me?"

"What?"

"A place where nobody looked at me like I was a problem."

Ryan nodded. "That matters."

"It mattered more than I knew at the time," Nick said. "I could walk in there and breathe. Be myself. People knew my name. Wanted me there."

Ryan smiled a little. "Sounds like home."

Nick looked back at him. "Yeah," he said quietly. "It did."

Ryan leaned back in his chair. "I get that now."

Nick studied him for a second before he asked, "And this place? Your house?"

Ryan frowned slightly. "What about it?"

Nick's voice lowered. "It's starting to feel like home too."

Ryan didn't answer right away. Something passed between them then—quiet and real and harder to joke away than either of them probably wanted to admit. He finally said, "Good."

Nick held his gaze a second longer than usual. Neither one of them looked away first.

From inside the house, Ryan's mom called out that they were probably grilling soon. Nick broke the moment with a grin.

"Well. Guess romance is dead. Burgers are calling."

Ryan laughed and tossed a towel at him. "You're an idiot."

"Maybe," Nick said, catching it. "But I'm your idiot for the afternoon."

Ryan shook his head, smiling despite himself. "Come on. Let's go eat."

As they headed inside, both of them knew something had shifted again. Not dramatically. Not loudly. Just enough that neither of them could pretend they didn't feel it.

Chapter 21
A Place at the Table

RYAN AND NICK LOUNGED OUTSIDE while the family moved around inside getting dinner ready. The smell drifting through the open patio door caught both their attention almost immediately. Whatever Ryan's mom was making, it was working.

Ryan laughed, stood, and grabbed a towel.

"I need to see what that is."

Nick stayed stretched out in the lounge chair a moment longer, enjoying the late sun, while Ryan headed inside.

He stepped into the kitchen and found his mother moving quickly between the stove and counter.

"What smells so good?"

She smiled without turning around. "Chicken in the oven, baked potatoes, salad, and a few other things. Thought I'd make a real dinner tonight."

"It smells incredible. Need help?"

Before she could answer, Nick came in through the patio door and stopped short.

"Oh wow. That smells amazing."

Ryan's mother laughed. "You two can smell food from a mile away."

Nick grinned. "That is absolutely true."

The counters were crowded with bowls, trays, and serving dishes. It looked like enough food for twice the number of people in the house, but Ryan knew his mother always cooked like that when she was happy.

He started setting drinks on the table, already knowing what everyone wanted without asking. Nick offered to help, but Ryan's mother waved him off.

"You can relax for five minutes. Dinner's almost done."

Nick nodded and wandered into the living room, where Kate sat cross-legged in front of the television, completely absorbed in a dance program.

He paused by the doorway.

"Hey, Kate. Mind if I join you?"

She looked up and smiled. "Okay. It's my ballerina show."

Nick sat beside her. "Then I'm honored."

Kate scooted over to make room.

"I want to be a ballerina one day," she said matter-of-factly.

Nick nodded seriously. "That sounds like a pretty great plan."

"You dance?"

"I do," he said. "Not ballet exactly. But I love dancing. Love music. Love performing."

Her eyes widened. "Really?"

"Really."

Kate beamed. "Ryan doesn't dance."

Nick laughed. "That is not entirely true. I've seen him try."

That got a genuine laugh from her.

"I like singing too," she said. "And animals."

"Strong combination," Nick replied. "You've got range."

From the hallway, Ryan stopped for a moment and watched them together. Nick was relaxed in a way Ryan hadn't seen often—easy, warm, completely natural. Kate, who usually took a while to warm up to people, looked like she'd known him for years.

Ryan smiled to himself and headed back to the kitchen.

His mother glanced at him. "What?"

"Nothing."

"That smile means something."

Ryan leaned against the counter. "What do you think of Nick?"

She didn't hesitate.

"I think he's sweet. I think he's had a hard life. And I think he's trying very hard not to show how much he appreciates being here."

Ryan looked down.

"Yeah," he said quietly. "That sounds right."

She lowered the heat on one burner and turned toward him.

"I also think you're different since he got here."

Ryan raised an eyebrow. "Different how?"

"Happier. Lighter. More yourself."

He looked away toward the living room.

"We just get along."

"I can see that."

Ryan hesitated before speaking more carefully.

"If he wanted to stay here through school… would that be okay?"

His mother softened immediately.

"Honey, we already told him he could."

"No, I mean really stay. Finish senior year. Live here."

She smiled. "If that's what he wants, yes. Your father feels the same way."

Ryan let out a breath he hadn't realized he was holding.

"I think it'd be good for him."

"I think so too," she said. "And I think it might be good for you."

Ryan rolled his eyes. "Don't start."

"I didn't say anything."

"You definitely did."

She laughed and handed him a stack of plates.

"Go tell everyone dinner's ready."

As Ryan turned toward the living room, the front door opened and his father walked in from work, loosening his tie.

"Something smells fantastic."

"Perfect timing," Ryan's mother called. "Wash up."

His father spotted Ryan.

"The boys staying for dinner?"

Ryan smirked. "Think so."

"Good."

In the living room, Kate and Nick were still watching television.

Ryan stood in the doorway. "Dinner's ready. Hands washed. Move it."

Kate groaned dramatically and got up.

Nick stood too. "Sorry. I got distracted."

Ryan shrugged. "She likes you."

Nick glanced toward Kate, then back at Ryan.

"I like her too."

Something about the simplicity of that landed with Ryan more than it should have.

They moved into the dining room together.

The table was fully set, the kind of meal Ryan's mother only made when she wanted everyone gathered in one place. Platters of chicken, bowls of salad, foil-wrapped potatoes, warm rolls, vegetables, drinks—everything arranged with more care than necessary.

Nick stopped in the doorway for a second and just stared.

Ryan noticed immediately.

"You okay?"

Nick blinked and smiled, though it looked emotional around the edges.

"Yeah. Just… wow."

They all sat down, passing dishes, filling plates, talking over each other the way families do when nobody is trying to impress anyone.

Nick moved slower than everyone else, taking it in. Ryan's mother noticed.

"Nick, is something wrong?"

Nick looked embarrassed for being noticed at all.

"Nothing. Just not used to this."

The room quieted slightly.

Ryan's father spoke first.

"Used to what?"

Nick glanced around the table.

"This. Everybody sitting down together. Real dinner. People wanting to be here."

No one rushed to fill the silence after that. Ryan's mother simply reached over and set another basket of rolls near him.

"Well," she said gently, "get used to it."

Nick laughed once, then looked down quickly. Ryan saw the shine in his eyes and looked away to give him dignity.

His mother continued like it was no big moment at all.

"As we've said," Ryan's mother continued nonchalantly as she put food on her plate, "you're welcome here as long as you need to be. Whether that's a week, the rest of summer, or until graduation. We mean that."

Nick swallowed hard.

"Thank you."

His father nodded once.

"House rules are simple. Be respectful, help out, and don't eat the last dessert without asking."

That got a laugh from everyone, including Nick.

"I can do that."

Dinner loosened after that. Stories were told. Kate talked about dance class she wanted to take. Ryan's father complained about traffic. Ryan's mother corrected half his story. Nick laughed more than he talked, but when he did speak, everyone listened.

By the time plates were empty, the room felt fuller than it had before dinner started.

Ryan sat back in his chair and watched Nick across the table. He fit here—not awkwardly, not temporarily, but naturally.

That realization stirred something in Ryan he wasn't ready to name. This wasn't just about helping somebody anymore. It wasn't charity. It wasn't convenience.

Nick mattered here.

And maybe, if Ryan was honest, he mattered to Ryan in a way that was getting harder to ignore.

Nick looked up and caught him staring. Ryan immediately reached for his drink like that had been his plan all along.

Nick hid a smile.

Across the table, Ryan's mother saw everything and said nothing, which for now felt like kindness.

Chapter 22
What She Carried

RYAN WENT UP TO HIS ROOM and crashed almost as soon as he hit the bed. The day had been long, heavier than he wanted to admit, but somehow good too. He had spent time with his family, spent time with Nick, and finally said things out loud that he had buried for more than a year.

It felt strange, letting someone else carry pieces of him like that. Not because he didn't trust Nick, but because he wasn't used to being that open without feeling like he had to defend himself afterward. With Nick, it had been different. He could say something ugly, confusing, or shameful, and Nick didn't turn it into an interrogation. He listened. He understood more than Ryan expected.

Across the hall, Nick lay on his bed staring at the ceiling, too overwhelmed to sleep right away. The house was quiet, but his mind wasn't. He kept thinking about dinner, about Ryan's family, about the way they had made room for him without making it feel like charity. They had taken him in, fed him, welcomed him, and somehow made him feel like he belonged.

That kind of love still felt unreal.

He turned onto his side and wiped at his eyes before the tears could really fall. He wasn't used to being wanted. Not like this. Not by people who expected nothing from him except that he stay safe and maybe be okay.

Then, without meaning to, his thoughts shifted to Ryan. There was something there, something Nick could feel even when neither of them said it. Maybe it was too soon. Maybe it was too complicated. Ryan was still figuring himself out, and Nick knew better than to rush that. Still, there were moments when Ryan looked at him and Nick felt it in his chest.

He had only felt something close to that once before, and it had turned into a mess. This felt different.

Eventually, exhaustion pulled him under.

By morning, the house had returned to its usual rhythm. Around seven, cabinets opened and closed, coffee brewed, and footsteps moved through the kitchen. Ryan was already downstairs with a mug in his hand when Nick came in, still sleepy but smiling.

"Good morning, all," Nick said.

"Morning," everyone answered in scattered voices.

Nick poured himself coffee and leaned against the counter for a second. "Last night was great," he said, looking around at them. "I just want to thank you all again. It means a lot to me. More than I probably know how to say."

Ryan's mom smiled warmly. "You're welcome, honey. You've become part of things around here, and we're glad you're here."

Nick looked down at his coffee, trying not to get emotional. "Thank you."

She gave him a moment before asking, "What are you boys doing today?"

Nick glanced at Ryan. "Maybe the beach again. Maybe stop by the club later. Not sure yet."

Ryan shrugged. "I'm good with the beach."

"Sounds good to me," Nick said.

They took their coffee out to the lanai, settling into the familiar quiet of the morning. The air was already humid, but the day was too nice to waste inside. Sitting out there had become part of their routine—coffee, sun, a few minutes of peace before the day started moving too fast.

Once they finished, they got ready and drove toward the beach. It felt like a normal morning, but as they got closer, Nick felt something shift. He couldn't place it. Maybe it was nothing. Maybe he was just tired from everything that had happened lately. Still, the feeling stayed with him.

They parked a couple blocks away and walked down to Ryan's usual spot. The beach was still fairly quiet, early enough that the heavier crowds hadn't arrived. The breeze off the ocean softened the heat, and the water looked bright and clean under the sun.

Ryan and Nick spread out their towels and settled in, both letting the calm take over for a while. There was no sign of Ryan's old friends, no drama waiting for them, no one calling his name from across the sand. For once, it seemed like the day might stay easy.

Then Nick saw her.

At first, she was just a figure walking along the edge of the water, close enough for him to notice but too far away to recognize. A woman, thin and unsteady, her clothes rumpled, her hair messy, her feet moving slowly through the surf. She looked out of place, like she had wandered there without fully knowing why.

Nick sat up, squinting behind his sunglasses.

Ryan noticed. "What?"

Nick didn't answer right away. The woman turned slightly, and his stomach dropped.

"Oh my God," he said. "Mom?"

Ryan sat up fast. "Wait. That's her?"

Nick stared, unable to move for a second. "Yeah. That's her. What the hell is she doing here?"

The woman kept walking, looking out at the water like she hadn't seen the ocean in years. Maybe she hadn't. Nick couldn't remember the last time she had gone anywhere just to breathe.

Ryan's voice stayed careful. "Do you want to go talk to her?"

Nick swallowed hard. "I don't know. She can be unpredictable. I don't know what she's on, or if she's on anything. I don't know what's happened since I left."

But he was already standing.

Ryan stayed back, watching as Nick walked toward the shoreline. Each step felt heavier than the last. By the time he caught up to her, his throat had gone tight.

"Mom?"

The woman turned slowly. Her eyes moved over his face without recognition at first, distant and foggy.

"Yes?" she said. "Who are you? Everything's a little fuzzy right now."

Nick felt something inside him crack. "Mom, it's me. Nick. Your son."

She stared at him, blinking. Then the name seemed to land.

"Nick," she whispered. "My son."

Her eyes filled almost immediately. She reached for him with shaking hands. "I told you to run. I told you to be free."

Nick stepped into her arms before he could stop himself. "I didn't go far. I still have to finish school. I've been staying with someone. Good people."

She held him tighter. "Good. That's good. I didn't want you in that house anymore. Not until things changed. Not until it was safe."

Nick pulled back enough to look at her. "I thought about coming by. I wanted to check on you. I just couldn't make myself do it yet."

"You shouldn't have," she said quickly. "Not yet. You did what you needed to do."

Nick searched her face. She looked exhausted, worn down, and older than he remembered. Still, there was something clearer in her eyes than he expected.

"How's Dad?" he asked.

Her expression changed. It was small, but Nick saw it.

"Mom," he said. "Where is he?"

She looked away toward the ocean. "He's gone."

Nick went still. "What does that mean?"

She took a shaky breath, eyes filling again. "The day you left… everything happened fast."

Nick stared at her, waiting.

"He was looking for you," she said. "Screaming for you. He had the belt. I knew what he was going to do if he found you."

Nick's hands curled at his sides.

"I tried to stop him," she continued. "He hit me. Knocked me down. I remember blood in my mouth and hearing him break through your door. I thought he had gotten to you."

Nick's voice dropped. "I was already climbing out."

"I know that now," she said. "But I didn't know then. I thought he was going to kill you one day, Nick. Maybe not that day, maybe not the next, but one day."

She looked at him then, and the truth sat between them before she even said it.

"I got the gun."

Nick barely breathed.

"He came at me," she said. "I told him to leave you alone. Told him you deserved better than us. He laughed at me. Said I wouldn't do anything."

Her voice trembled, but she kept going.

"The first time, it didn't fire. Safety was on. He lunged at me, and then…" She closed her eyes briefly. "Then it did."

Nick stared at her. The beach noise faded around him.

"You shot him?"

She nodded once, barely. "Yes."

"Is he dead?"

Her face crumpled. "Yes."

For a few seconds, Nick couldn't speak. He looked out at the water, then back at her, trying to make the words mean something. His father was gone. Really gone. The man who had made him afraid to sleep, afraid to come home, afraid to exist, would never touch him again.

He should have felt only relief. He didn't.

In addition to the relief, a myriad of emotions turned in his stomach: grief, shock, anger, and something hollow all at once.

"Why didn't you just leave?" Nick asked. "Why didn't you make him leave?"

"Because he always came back," she said. "And I knew he would come back for you."

Nick looked down at the sand.

"I called 911 after," she said. "I told them the truth. Enough of it. He attacked me. I defended myself."

Nick looked at her sharply. "Are you in trouble?"

"No," she said. "Not right now. There was enough history. Enough proof." She swallowed. "But that house is still full of everything we were. I'm trying to get clean. I'm trying, Nick. I'm not ready for you to come back. Not yet."

Nick's eyes burned. "You're still my mom."

"I know," she whispered. "And that's why I need you to stay away until I can be better than I was."

He wanted to argue. He wanted to tell her he could help. But some part of him knew she was right. He had spent years taking care of people who should have taken care of him.

He couldn't go back to that.

"I'm safe," he said finally. "I'm happy. I'm staying with Ryan and his family. They're good to me."

Her shoulders loosened, like that was the one thing she had needed to hear. "Then stay there. Finish school. Be something. Please."

Nick nodded, tears falling now. "I love you."

She pulled him into another hug. "I love you too. More than I knew how to show."

For a while, they just stood there.

Then Nick looked back toward Ryan, who was watching from a distance but giving them space. Nick wiped his face and turned to his mother.

"I want you to meet him."

She followed his gaze. "Ryan?"

"Yeah," Nick said. "He's my friend."

They walked back together. Ryan stood as they approached, his expression open but careful.

"Ryan," Nick said, his voice still rough, "this is my mom. Mom, this is Ryan."

Ryan extended his hand. "Hi. I'm Ryan."

She took it gently. "Terri. It's nice to meet you."

"You too," Ryan said. "I'm glad you're okay. Nick's been worried about you."

Terri looked at Nick, then back at Ryan. "Thank you for helping him."

Ryan didn't make a big thing of it. "He's helped me too."

That seemed to touch her. She nodded; eyes damp again.

"I should go," she said after a moment. "I need to keep moving."

Nick's face tightened. "Where are you going?"

"Back," she said. "For now. I have things to do. Things to fix. But not you. You are not something I get to fix by dragging you back."

Nick looked like that hurt and helped at the same time.

"One day," she said, touching his cheek. "Give me time. If I get myself together, maybe we can talk more. Maybe we can start again somehow."

Nick nodded. "Okay."

Terri hugged him one last time, holding on like she didn't want to let go but knew she had to. Then she stepped back.

"Take care of him," she said to Ryan.

"I will," Ryan said.

She gave Nick one last look. "Be free."

Then she turned and walked down the beach.

Nick watched her until she grew smaller in the distance. He didn't move for a long time. Ryan came up beside him and rested a hand on his shoulder, not pushing, not asking too much.

"I'm glad you saw her," Ryan said quietly.

Nick nodded, still staring after her. "Me too."

"You okay?"

Nick let out a breath that almost shook. "I don't know. My dad's dead."

Ryan didn't say anything.

“I thought I’d feel happy,” Nick said. “Part of me does. I hate that, but I do. He can’t hurt me anymore. He can’t hurt her anymore. But it’s still… I don’t know. It’s still my dad.”

Ryan squeezed his shoulder once. “That makes sense.”

Nick looked down at the sand. “She saved me. Too late, maybe, but she did. And now she’s trying to save herself.”

“Maybe that’s the start,” Ryan said.

“Maybe.” Nick wiped at his face, then looked back at the water. “I don’t know if I can forgive her.”

“You don’t have to decide that today.”

Nick nodded slowly. “Yeah.”

They sat back down on the towels, quieter now. The beach was still beautiful, the waves still rolling in, the sun still bright overhead. Everything looked the same, even though nothing felt the same anymore.

After a while, they packed up to leave. Before they walked back to the car, Nick stopped and looked out at the ocean one more time. For the first time, his past felt a little farther away. Not gone, but farther.

Ryan glanced at him, then gave him a small smile. Nick managed one back, and then they walked off the beach together.

Chapter 23
The Last Invitation

RYAN WOKE TO THE BUZZ OF HIS PHONE, on the nightstand, and reached for it without opening his eyes. When he finally looked at the screen, he saw a text from Jim.

Hope to see you tomorrow evening at the party.

Ryan stared at it longer than he expected. Jim sounded excited, almost too excited, which made Ryan wonder if there was some angle behind it. Then again, maybe there wasn't. Maybe Jim really did just want him there for one last party before everyone scattered to college and whatever came next.

Still, nothing involving that group was ever simple.

Part of him thought going might be good. Seeing Julie in a normal setting could clear the air. Maybe one final night together as a group could close things better than they had ended.

Another part of him knew how fast those nights could go wrong.

He thought about last summer, about drinking too much, crossed lines, and chaos disguised as fun. After a moment, he typed back.

Sounds good. See you then.

He tossed the phone aside and got up for a run.

A few minutes later, he knocked on Nick's door. Nick answered almost immediately, hair messy and eyes half-open.

"You dragging me out already?" Nick asked.

Ryan smirked. "You coming or not?"

Nick stretched and yawned. "Yeah. Give me thirty seconds."

They headed out together, jogging through the neighborhood before cutting into the busier streets closer to town. The city was already awake—delivery trucks unloading, store owners opening up, dog walkers, cyclists, early traffic rolling through intersections.

Running there was different than running near home. There was more noise, more movement, and more things demanding your attention. It also made the miles pass faster.

They raced each other down one long stretch, laughing when Ryan nearly clipped a newspaper stand trying to pass Nick.

"Real graceful," Nick called out.

"Still beat you," Ryan shot back.

"You absolutely did not."

They slowed near a corner, both catching their breath.

"You cheat," Nick said.

"I'm naturally gifted."

"You're naturally full of shit."

They laughed again and started back toward the house. A few blocks away, Ryan slowed to a stop.

Nick looked over. "What's up?"

Ryan hesitated. "I want to stop by Julie's before I head home. Just for a few minutes."

Nick studied him. "You okay going alone?"

"Yeah," Ryan said. "I just want to talk about tomorrow."

Nick nodded once. "All right. If Zach's there, don't kill him."

Ryan snorted. "I'll show restraint."

"Big personal growth."

Ryan shoved him lightly. "Get out of here."

Nick grinned and jogged off toward the house while Ryan turned toward Julie's.

He slowed when her house came into view.

He had spent so much time there once that walking up now felt strange. There had been afternoons by the pool, dinners with her family, late-night kisses by the back gate, fights in the driveway, apologies in the kitchen.

Now it felt like someone else's life.

Ryan rang the bell, and the housekeeper answered with a warm smile.

"Ah, Señor Ryan. How are you?"

"I'm good," he said. "Is Julie around?"

"Yes. Come in. She is by the pool."

Ryan thanked her and walked through the house, noticing how everything looked the same while feeling completely different. He stepped outside and found Julie stretched out in a lounge chair, tanning in the morning sun.

She lowered her sunglasses when she saw him.

"Ryan," she said. "What are you doing here?"

"Hey, Julie."

He stayed standing.

"I came to talk about tomorrow."

"The party?"

"Yeah. Jim texted me. Said I should come."

"And?"

"And I wanted to make sure you were okay with it."

Julie gave a faint smile. "Ryan, there are going to be a hundred people here. You showing up won't shake the earth."

"That's not what I meant."

"I know what you meant."

She motioned toward the chair beside her.

"Sit down or loom dramatically. Your choice."

Ryan stayed where he was.

She sighed. "Still stubborn."

He ignored that. "I wanted to know where we stand."

Julie sat up slowly. "We broke up. That's where we stand."

"You know what I mean."

"Then say what you actually came here to say."

Ryan exhaled. "Last summer's party got out of hand. A lot of things happened that shouldn't have happened."

Julie's expression hardened. "You were there too."

"I know I was there."

"You participated."

"I got dragged into a lot of shit."

Julie laughed once, sharp and humorless. "Dragged?"

Ryan's jaw tightened. "You always do that. You act like I was the only one who made mistakes."

"No," she said coolly. "I act like you never own yours."

"That's bullshit."

"Is it?"

They stared at each other.

Ryan stepped closer. "I'm not doing this blame game again. I came here because I'm thinking of bringing Nick tomorrow, and I want to know if people are going to act like idiots."

Julie's eyes narrowed. "So this is about Nick."

"It's about all of it."

She leaned back in the chair. "No one cares as much as you think they do."

"Zach does."

Julie looked away for a second. "Zach can be handled."

Ryan barked a short laugh. "Can he?"

"Yes."

"Since when?"

"Since I said so."

Ryan shook his head. "That's exactly what I mean. You always think you can control everything."

"And you always think everything happens to you."

"That's rich coming from you."

Julie stood now, anger rising.

"You came to my house to insult me?"

"I came here trying to be civil."

"No, Ryan. You came here suspicious, angry, and looking for a fight."

"I came here because I know how this group works."

Julie crossed her arms. "Maybe you're worried because secrets don't stay buried forever."

That landed harder than he expected.

Ryan's voice dropped. "What does that mean?"

"Maybe nothing."

"No. What do you know?"

Julie shrugged. "I know you better than you think."

"You know nothing."

"Do I?"

Ryan felt heat rise in his chest. "If you have something to say, say it."

Julie stepped closer.

"You spent half our relationship pretending. Pretending to be fine. Pretending to want things you didn't want. Pretending to love me the way I loved you."

"That's not fair."

"It's true."

"I did love you."

"In the way you could," she said. "But even then, something was always missing."

Ryan looked away.

Julie's voice softened only slightly.

"I knew before you did."

He turned back sharply. "Knew what?"

"That you were fighting yourself."

The words stunned him more than if she had screamed.

"You should've told me," he said quietly.

Julie's eyes flashed. "That wasn't my truth to tell."

They stood in silence for a beat before Ryan hardened again.

"So instead you punished me."

Julie scoffed. "You really think everything is punishment."

"I think you know how to hurt people when you want to."

"And I think you know how to disappear while standing right in front of someone."

Ryan took a step back.

"Fine," he said. "I'll come tomorrow."

Julie picked up her sunglasses.

"Do what you want."

He started toward the door, then turned once more.

"You still never answered me."

"About what?"

"Can Nick trust being there?"

Julie held his gaze. "More than I could trust you."

Ryan laughed bitterly. "Still cruel."

"And you're still dramatic."

He shook his head. "Unbelievable."

"Then leave."

Ryan walked away.

Behind him, Julie called out, "See you tomorrow, Ryan."

He didn't answer.

By the time he got home, the anger had worn off and left only exhaustion.

He dropped into a chair near the pool and stared at the water until Nick came outside carrying two drinks. Nick handed one over and sat beside him.

"So," Nick said. "How'd it go?"

Ryan took a sip first. "Badly."

Nick nodded. "That sounds right."

Ryan let out a breath. "She said the party's fine. She said nobody's going to start anything."

"And you believe that?"

"No."

Nick leaned back. "What else?"

Ryan hesitated. "She knows more than she lets on."

"About you?"

"Yeah."

Nick was quiet for a moment. "Does that scare you?"

Ryan thought about it. "Maybe."

Nick nudged his shoulder lightly.

"You know what I think?"

"What?"

"I think tomorrow is going to be chaos either way."

Ryan laughed despite himself. "Helpful."

"I try."

Ryan looked over at him. "I kind of wish you wouldn't come."

Nick raised an eyebrow. "Not happening."

"Nick."

"I can handle myself."

"That's not the point."

"Then what is?"

Ryan didn't answer immediately.

Finally he said, "I don't want you getting dragged into my mess."

Nick's expression softened.

"Too late," he said. "I like your mess."

Ryan shook his head, smiling despite himself.

"You're insane."

"Probably."

They sat together in the afternoon heat, both pretending not to think about tomorrow.

Neither of them was fooling the other.

The party would be the last one of its kind. It would be the end of something old before everyone moved on to whatever came next.

Neither of them knew how much could change in one night.

That evening, Ryan lay in bed staring at the ceiling.

He replayed every word Julie had said.

I knew before you did.

He didn't know whether that made him angry, embarrassed, or relieved.

Outside his room, the house had gone quiet. Tomorrow could be fun, or tomorrow could be a disaster.

Ryan had the sinking feeling it would be both.

Chapter 24
The Last Party

THE DAY OF JULIE'S END-OF-SUMMER PARTY finally arrived.

It was always the biggest party of the year, the one everyone talked about before school started again. Julie never did anything halfway, and this year was no different. If anything, she had gone bigger than ever—catered food, kegs, good liquor, music, lights, and enough people invited that the house would be packed before the sun even went down.

For years, Ryan had helped her with it. He had been part of the planning, part of the setup, part of the whole image. This time, he wasn't co-hosting anything. He was just another guest, and that bothered him more than he wanted to admit.

At Julie's house, everything was already being arranged. Servers moved in and out, setting out trays and stocking coolers while music equipment was tested near the pool. Zach, meanwhile, had claimed a lounge chair and seemed perfectly content to watch everyone else work.

Julie glanced over at him, annoyed. "You know, Zach, you could help."

He lifted his sunglasses just enough to look at her. "Why? You've got people for that."

"You could at least check the kegs."

"I'll check them when the party starts," he said with a grin. "That's my job. Getting things going."

Julie rolled her eyes, though she was smiling a little. "That's what you and Ryan were always good at."

Zach's grin sharpened. "Yeah. Except tonight it's my show."

Julie gave him a look. "Don't do anything we'll regret."

"I can't promise that," he said. "But I can promise it won't be boring."

Julie didn't answer right away. She looked out over the pool, the setup, the house filling with the first signs of the night ahead. "Good," she said finally. "If this is the last one, it needs to be unforgettable."

Zach sat up, smirking. "Trust me. It will be."

Across town, Ryan started the day with a run, this time alone. He needed the space. He needed the quiet. Most of all, he needed time to get his head straight before walking into Julie's house again.

He told himself he was going to have fun. He told himself nothing had to happen. But he knew that group. He knew how they worked. Every party had a target. Every joke had an edge. Every time things went too far, someone laughed and called it tradition.

Back at home, Nick spent most of the day lounging by the pool, headphones in, sun on his skin, looking almost irritatingly calm. Ryan envied that. Nick didn't seem scared of the party at all, but Ryan knew better. Nick had survived worse, and maybe that was why he wasn't afraid.

Ryan's mom noticed the tension anyway.

"Sounds like you boys have a party tonight," she said from the kitchen.

"Yeah," Ryan replied. "Julie's."

She studied him for a moment. "Be careful. I know things are complicated with you two right now."

"I know."

"If anything feels wrong, you can always come home. There's no shame in leaving."

Ryan nodded. "Thanks, Mom."

She smiled gently. "Try to enjoy yourself too. This may be the last time you see some of them for a while."

"I'll try."

Ryan went outside and found Nick still stretched out by the pool.

"You ready for this party?" Ryan asked.

Nick pushed his sunglasses up. "Yeah. I think it'll be fun."

"You're way too calm."

Nick shrugged. "If it gets weird, we leave. Simple."

Ryan wished it felt that simple.

By early evening, Ryan was dressed and pacing the kitchen with a drink in his hand. He checked his phone, texted Jim that they were heading over soon, and tried not to look as nervous as he felt.

Then Nick came downstairs.

He wasn't dressed too flashy, but he looked sharp—clean, confident, hair styled with just enough shine to catch the light. Ryan looked at him a second too long.

"You look good," Ryan said.

Nick smiled. "Yeah?"

"Yeah. Really good."

"Figured I should make a decent impression."

Ryan handed him a bottle of water. "Drink that first. Then we'll go."

Nick took it, still smiling. "Yes, Dad."

Ryan shook his head. "Shut up."

Since Julie lived close, they walked. It made more sense than driving, especially with drinking involved, and there would already be too many cars lining the street. As they got closer, they could hear the music before they reached the house.

Julie's party was already alive.

People spilled through the front door, gathered along the driveway, and crowded the backyard. Lights glowed around the pool, drinks were everywhere, and the bass from the speakers pulsed through the warm night air.

Jim spotted them almost immediately.

"Ryan!" he called, weaving through the crowd. "You made it."

"I said I would."

Jim glanced at Nick. "And you brought your friend. Nick, right?"

Nick nodded. "Yeah. We met at the burger place."

"Good to see you, man. You want a beer?"

"Sure."

Jim grabbed beers for both of them, and they toasted quickly before Ryan started scanning the crowd. He found Julie near the pool, and Zach wasn't far from her.

Of course he wasn't.

A few minutes later, the music cut out and Zach climbed onto a low wall near the pool.

"Yo! Shut the hell up for a second!" he shouted.

The crowd responded with cheers, whistles, and raised cups.

Zach lifted his drink. "First off, everybody better thank Julie for throwing the best damn party of the summer."

More cheering followed.

Julie smiled, playing the part perfectly while Zach continued louder now. "This is the last one before everybody heads off and pretends to grow up. So let's make it count. Drink, dance, do something stupid—but don't be boring."

The crowd roared as the music blasted back on, louder than before.

Ryan watched from the side, jaw tight.

Nick leaned closer. "You okay?"

"Yeah," Ryan said. "Just watching the performance."

Ryan eventually made his way toward Julie with Nick beside him.

"Great party," Ryan said. "You really went all out."

Julie smiled, but there was something guarded behind it. "I had to. It's the last one."

"Yeah. I figured."

Her eyes flicked toward Nick, then back to Ryan. "Glad you came."

"Are you?"

"Ryan."

Before she could say more, Zach appeared beside her, still riding the high of the crowd.

"Well, look at this," he said. "Ryan decided to come home."

Ryan kept his expression flat. "Nice speech."

Zach grinned. "Jealous?"

"Of what?"

"Me standing where you used to."

Ryan glanced around. "You mean near the alcohol, taking credit for work you didn't do?"

Julie's smile dropped slightly.

Zach laughed, but his eyes hardened. "Careful. Night's young."

"I'm aware."

Zach looked at Nick. "You having fun yet?"

Nick gave him a polite smile. "So far."

"Good. Stick around. It gets better."

Ryan didn't like the way he said it.

"We're going to play beer pong," Ryan said, stepping away before Zach could push harder.

Nick followed him toward the tables where Jim and a few others had already set up a game. People recognized Ryan immediately. Some greeted him like nothing had changed. Others stared at Nick with open curiosity.

"So who's this?" one guy asked.

"Nick," Ryan said. "He's a friend."

Nick lifted a hand. "Hey."

"You play?"

"Never played this version," Nick said. "But I'll try."

That was all it took.

Within ten minutes, Nick was winning.

At first, people laughed because he was new. Then they started watching because he was good. Cup after cup, he hit his shots, and the crowd around the table grew louder with every round.

Ryan couldn't help smiling.

Nick was flushed from the beer and the attention, but he looked happy. Not guarded. Not careful. Just happy. For a while, the party felt almost normal.

Then Zach showed up.

"I'll play him," he said, stepping into the circle. "Might as well see if the new guy's actually good."

Ryan looked at Nick. "You sure?"

Nick nodded. "Yeah. I'm sure."

Zach grinned. "Bold."

Nick picked up the ball. "You talk a lot."

The crowd reacted with laughter and cheers.

Zach's smile thinned. "Throw."

Nick did.

He hit the cup. Then another. Then another.

Zach drank each time, keeping his expression loose, but Ryan could see the irritation building. Zach didn't like being beaten. He liked it even less when people cheered for someone else.

By the final round, Nick was swaying a little, but he was still focused. Zach had one cup left. Nick sank his last shot and lifted both hands as the crowd erupted.

Zach missed.

The reaction was immediate—cheers, laughter, people shouting Nick's name. For one bright second, Nick looked stunned by it. Then he laughed, soaking it in.

Zach laughed too.

But his laugh was wrong.

"Good job," Zach said, clapping slowly. "Really. Impressive."

Nick set the ball down. "Good game."

"Don't walk off yet," Zach said.

Nick paused. "Why?"

"I have a surprise."

Ryan felt his stomach drop.

Nick's smile faded. "I'm good."

Zach's voice sharpened. "No, you're not. Stay where you are."

Ryan stepped forward. "Zach."

Zach ignored him and looked at Nick. "You think you can walk in here, take Ryan with you, make everyone cheer for you, and then just leave?"

Nick stared at him. "Ryan makes his own choices."

"Oh, does he?" Zach laughed. "That's cute."

Ryan moved between them. "Back off."

LADLE AND CUP

1956. A pot of water
simmers over flame, the bubbles
first slow then rapid
burst, break surface tension

a green pod brews   unseals
itself, exhales a gas. (Other hands
have ground such pods with pestles
to powder, disguised the bitter taste
in buttered roti, laddu
Boldly scattered them to rats   starving
mongrels)

the water is the colour
of tea. One hand holds a ladle
the other, a tin cup.   Whose heart
commands these hands?

DUKH

Piari Speaks:

I am seven when I died. I love
my oldest brother best. Drank tea from a cup that makes
my inside hard and green, twist
in half on the ground. I am sleep, my dukh, *my sorrow, I am calling*
for my mother

Piara:

I can remember her
playing in the pond
and once we ate a watermelon together
in a field
she showed me how to break it open
in half, on the ground

Shivani:

Wake, my daughter, my *beti,* beloved one
It is your mother who falls beside you
in half, on the ground

ॐ

A farmer saw Piari often on the outskirts of the mango grove weeks after she had died. The first time he glimpsed her it was still monsoon, the rain too heavy for his eyes to navigate the drops; he half thought she was a lost bull calf. He swung his head back and forth like a peacock in heat, held his hands in front of him as though he could part the storm. He rode his buffalo toward her blurred image and it was afraid to go.

It was months later that he bolted into the village, eyes so strange it was like they had melted from staring at intense heat, so that the colours began to run, brown into white. He'd been gone for three nights, telling his wife he would sleep under the sky now that the rains had passed. When he came running, Piara and Aaj were walking the wall by the pond. They watched him get closer, his legs kicking up in the tall grass, red tunic sliding off his shoulders. A piece of iron chain in his hand, swinging. They watched for the thing that must be chasing him to appear—the flash of a long tooth, the wink of a stripe. A forked tongue.

He came to them screaming, rousing sleeping cows. He described her face, her throat swollen with poison, peeking out from around a mango tree. Her eyes beckoning. *She curls on my chest in the night,* he howled, *I wake up and cannot get a breath.* It is like so many stones.

The village seers grasped him by the arms, dragged him to Piari's grave. They meant to beat him with the iron chain to loose her spirit. *It is no good,* he said. *I have already beaten myself.* They lifted off his shirt to see the blood, pooling in the link marks on his back. He stayed there, writhing on her grave through the night. Sometimes he called her name, like a lover's.

FLOUR (II)

Aaj:

We stole from the grainhouse, everybody
did it. One handful in the fold of a tunic, one
in your pocket. Somebody watching outside to say
Auntie is coming. Chaginder was the worst,
he brought a bowl with him, pulled it out
of his trousers and filled it with corn, ran down
the street trying not to spill. I walked slowly, kept my wheat
in cupped hands, careful, away from the wind

We stood in groups outside the alley-shop, faces
hopeful, hands held out to the man
who squatted down to weigh each stolen grain
picking them out of his long yellowed beard
when they fell. Some days he gave us humbugs, some days
licorice. Once he had a glass jar of peppermints, white, smooth
sugary-cold. We sucked them on our backs
in the mustard fields and laughed, blew
our breath in each other's faces

The year there was drought
none of us would dare. Each day the village men farmed
invisible crops—more sweat than food
We watched our mothers bent on the grainhouse floor, the folds
of their kameezes empty, watched them scrape the bottoms
of flour sacks with tin spoons. I went to the fields each day
carried home my wheat in cupped hands, careful,
away from the wind. At night
I dreamed of Chaginder's bowl overflowing
and the taste of peppermint

HEX

Piara comes down the street
from the sugar mill
scraps of cane husk caught
in the collar of his shirt, nine years old and drunk
for the first time on moonshine
Hey Chaginder
Smacks the rump of Mrs. Kumari's cow, spits
in the sewer ditch   *Chaginder get out here*
and fight you fat kauva, *can't put*
a hex on me!

From the courtyard men laugh, their kurtas
dirty from a day of labour
pass a long-necked pipe between them
Sundar's boy, they call, *whose bottle*
have you sipped from?

RATTLE

Shivani:

Piari was buried and Piara's sickness came
I saw it writhe in the soil, slide toward him
It came from the ground, from the grave
Like a lithe *shaa*, great *Supp*, diamond-backed
it crept up the leg of his white funeral pants

When I was a girl
my mother wouldn't let me walk
to school alone, past the sugar cane
where *Supp* slept in a black coil, waiting
to wrap himself around my legs
stick his double tongue in my soft ear
I wore bells on my ankles, stomped
like a boy past the sweet green stalks and
said my prayers

When I saw Piara's sickness come
I knew at once
Tore the bells from my ankles to shake them
rattle the shadow from my son

PIARI'S CREMATION

Aaj:

I was too young when she died
but I remember they always
told you not to look
too hard at the fire, or
the souls of the burning dead would enter
through your eyes

Piara:

I must've seen her
burning at the cremation site
I can't remember but I must've
they always made you watch
that kind of thing

*

Back

Ganesh, Ganesh, bo-besh, banana-fana fo-fesh, me my mo-mesh, Ganesh

ॐ

(Tell no one. This secret is for you alone.)
I told it all, of course. In front of my grade one
class I stood at the blackboard with empty hands, no
tail-feathers, not
a single whisker. They believed me anyway, drew tigers at lunchtime
with orange and black crayons, took a piece
of my secret garden home with them, to their dinner tables
to their beds and dreams. *Give it back,* I whispered
but they didn't hear
Give me back my India

FOR MY GREAT-GRANDFATHER

Like all the others
you came on a dark ship, followed
the beaten road from Port Victoria
to the camps and mills. Moore-Whittington
and BCFP, you worked
the greenchain for a dime
an hour, one dollar a day, until injury
prevented you. After
it was sparkwatch—face
inches from the kilns. Anyone I ask tells me

The same immigrant tale: *He walked*
to the camps at dawn, and home
at dusk, he never
missed a single day. Even when
it took the fingers from his hand he wanted
back on the chain, worked
with a hand and a half
to bring us across the sea. He kept the coin safe
and his own council safer, lived
simply. One egg
and a page of the Gita each morning
corn rotis and a pile of wood in winter
to keep out snow. Pay respect. He was buried
with honour. Because of this

I will never know you, mark
your mind from all the others, brown
sweat and ache, endless
chain of sums:
the price of passage
plus two-hundred, times two
times three   tickets for a silver plane
Divide by dimes
and hours   weeks   months   mouths
tent into shack into house
chickens to curry, school clothes
and books from Hudson's Bay   slivers and limbs, another
day with your face
inches from the kilns

I will pay my respect. Every hair, tooth and nail I owe
to you. But still
I long to pull the splinters, brush
the sawdust off
and wipe your brow. Who
would I see?

FOR MY GRANDFATHER (I)

When I was young I was so afraid of you
your plastic stomach, prosthetic
carapace with straps that hooked
through the belt loops of your pants, hard white shell
like a helmet. It hid
my horror: the great breathing
ball of red flesh encased in blue vein
your throbbing second heart

After the operation
when you were still drinking, you would knock
on your belly with your fists and your body
sounded hollow, the echo-ous
trip-trapping tarzan-man, and I
moved even closer to my mother
trying to be silent, trying to shut out
the noise, that terrible
empty baby kicking inside you

When you went back to the hospital
they took your scotch away forever.
I was older then, nine, old enough
to know you breathed your poison
in to my father's throat
while you lay there, sent it traveling
curls of gaseous fog
in to his mouth, his lungs
You turned his insides green with alcohol
in one sick breath. I saw it, your second heart
shuddered beneath the sheet
and beat, beat
beat

THE TREES IN THAT COUNTRY

All you taught me were numbers
Count to ten,
I can still do it

Show me a tree. In English: green
brown, root, trunk, bark, branch
leaf, flower
fruit on the bough, fruit on the ground
I picture Okanagan apple orchards
Nanoose Arbutus. West Coast Spruce and Oak
Show me a tree, dad

You struggle, your mouth shifting to that
other language. Those soft j's and hard ee's
n's that don't exist on the page. I know
there are words for trees in this tongue, words
that say things I can never understand
foreign pictures

In my head a Douglas Fir
grows in the centre of a Jalandhar field, its footing
in sugar cane soil. I am
tired of language, of my trapped tongue
in its crude patterns. Why give me
those ten numbers? Tiny things
for the wide inner spaces I saved, ten needles
on an empty pine tree—
were these all
you could spare?

ॐ

Once in the market outside Pubwan there was a traveling photographer who took a picture of the children for eight rupees. It survives in my Mahnji's house on Blackhall Street: her daughter and two sons benched in a neat row. Aaj and Piara are on the left and right in their white cotton shirts, clear smiling faces. But an accident must have happened. Above Piari's head a crack is superimposed—a complex rip radiating out from her temple in the black exposure, webbed pattern of white veins. *Or radiating in:* a shard of mirror about to impact.

She died days after the photograph was taken.

I have stared at this picture on the mantel in its glass frame, tried to erase the lines that distort her, never able to see her face whole

FOR MY GRANDMOTHER

You cook in an almond kitchen. Curry smells
cling to the walls, the furniture. This is the same chair
I have always sat in—white vinyl with yellow flowers;
the same banana and apple in a wicker bowl. Bells
on your ankles flash as you bend,
scoop flour with a tin cup

Your life has been a bending down
Your muscles move easily that way
humbled. Picking wheat, onions
lifting babies, your face
to the man you married

How do you cook like that, weed
the gardens in those yards of patterned
silk? Gold chains, bracelets, bells. How
can you bend so low
and not topple?

Your body is the dam
in the river; you

brace

yourself, hands buried

in a muddy bank

eyes squeezed tight

Stopping

the flood of progress

My Mahnji

What was it like to lose a child?
Your oldest daughter poisoned, asleep
in a green death. How did you grieve?
The rest of your babies have grown
and married this country, taught
their own daughters to do the same
Are we weak to you? Canadian

women climbing the hills of industry
embracing our isolation

THE GOOD WIFE

My father's betrothed, her picture hung on the wall
of the house in Pubwan and later, was put in a suitcase, crossed
the ocean and stood on my grandparents' mantel. Even at twelve
her face was plain; eyes too close together, too
low down on the forehead. She had a weak chin, wide
gaps between her teeth. *Aachaa,* Mahnji said
She will make a good wife

The picture remained through my father's
high school days, even after he'd learned
to say his plurals perfectly, read out lines
from Coleridge and then later Ginsberg without an accent
He wore tight pants, open-necked shirts
drove a car with shag on the steering wheel, big
back seat. *Aachaa,* Mahnji said
You need a good wife

She stayed on that mantle for years, face fixed
in the same plain smile, even after my parents were married
stayed long enough for me to be born
grow up and wonder
who she was. Later I learned that Mahnji
had finally sent a letter to the homeland:

> *My son*
> *has lost his mind, will bring no good*
> *to your family name. Please tell your daughter*
> *not to waste her time and wait, Acchaa*
> *she will make someone else*
> *a good wife*

KURDMYEE

The year I turned ten
my auntie Tage hid with my mother in the cloakroom
of the Guru Nanak Temple on Blackwood Street
wearing slippers of the softest silk
Gold tasseling, pale rubies sewn
to her scarlet sari, bangles clanking on her slender wrists
nose and ear connected
by a diamond chain
and *surma* sliding down her wet face

I kept watch for Mahnji at the cloakroom door, balanced
on the piles of big black shoes, camel-hair coats spilling out
into the arched hall
If this will make you miserable
my mother said to Tage, *then you shouldn't*
go through with it

Upstairs in the *Gurdwara,* the holy room
each relative touched forehead to floor
threw hundred dollar bills
into a brass trough at the foot of the altar
carved with wooden lotus

In the cloakroom, the sound of Tage's weeping
in the hall, noises from the temple kitchen
preparations for a feast—deep pots
full of chickpea, coconut rice
Trays of *jalebi* and *laddu*
pakora and *roti*
being stacked on the counters

I saw Mahnji's red *chunni* first
as she swept around the corner, I
turned fast, lost my footing. *She's coming*

My mother and I watched Tage run
to the parking lot, tassels flying
behind her like shining stocks of wheat
her heart beating in our hands

FOR MY GREAT-GRANDMOTHER

Old Mahnji Lali, always seemly
your tattoos
were a childhood riddle
Deep blue ink absorbed
by your tissue skin, the pictures
long ago feathered with age
The first time I saw them
I was eight, kneeling on the kitchen stool
elbows on the gold-flecked melamine
of your sink counter. You pushed
up the white sleeves of your cardigan
and I glimpsed the strange dye
before your arms were plunged
into dish soap bubbles. For years after
I waited for you to push up your sleeves

At eleven I had a vision
you as a girl
standing in an Indian temple
held down by priests
who drew symbols of your new womanhood
with cobalt needles and chanted
in Hindi, your
eyes squeezed tight and tears
greyed by surma
staining your gold-thread sari

When I was sixteen
I watched at Sarjaa's bhangra
while you danced
bare arms over your head
the blue ink peeking out
from between bouncing bangles
in the dance floor light
hands twisting like swan's necks

Two years later, a grown woman
I had enough courage,
finally to ask
while you lay in the hospital
healing from a broken rib
  I touched them
  your blue tattoos
and I asked

I was a young woman, you said
and every dry season in Jasomajara
the carnival would come
I went with my best girls and we all
got tattoos

the man that did mine was handsome
and I giggled so my arms shook
while he worked
I was always punished after—
my mother would smack my face
But every dry season
I would go again
and get another

You smiled an unseemly smile
and ran your skinny finger over
each cerulean story

This is a flower
This is a peacock
This is my name

FOR MY GRANDFATHER (II)

You went to England and
left a hole in my history
stretches of sub-continents,
immasculine time. Your face
interrupts my hot climates, mud
huts; you hang in a snowy split-screen
Southhall fashion. Blow freezing rain
into Jalandhar's red dust

You are non-essential. The Pubwan
seasons go by, drought and blood and
love. It is Mahnji who bears children, throws
dirt on their graves. She keeps
her eyes level with the seam of the land
searching for your clean winter

Years later my father went to London
and tried to piece you together

ॐ

Piara:

There's this bar in Southhall next to a Laundromat—
the beer tastes like soap. I met Uncle Jaal there for drinks
and I asked him about my dad, about the six missing
years, the time we guess at
when he was far away, working in London. Jaal is old
(the last one alive who can tell me) he can't remember
much, and it's almost too late

Jaal:

Sundar always wore a nice suit, you know, I never
saw him in poor clothes. He had his shoes custom
made in Auldgate. Once he came for dinner
and brought the girls a present each. Silver bangles

We sat across from each other at the wood table
Jaal in an old tweed suit jacket
cigarette burns on the lapels, blowing smoke in my face
He ordered more beer because
I was paying
He was there that night my dad was stabbed; I asked him
to tell me what happened and he told me

We were in a bar and Sundar had just got a letter
from your mother, I don't know what it said, but
he was drinking and drinking
He had a mug and it was half full of scotch. I don't
remember what happened but there was a fight
and he picked up a barstool

Jaal leaned in, his breath like bad milk

He hit this guy with a stool and the guy pulled a knife
small blade and jabbed it in
Sundar stood there with the knife in his stomach
somehow he still fought, smashed in a jaw, a nose—
he picked the guy up

Jaal told me

He threw him down the stairs. Broke
his neck. Sundar pulled out
the knife himself, that's all I know

Piara:

For all of my life I will write that letter in my head, the one
my dad was reading before he became a killer. Sometimes it says
Piari is dead and these are the times I love my dad
and think it was only the drink and that he was so blind with grief
he could break a man's neck
And sometimes the letter says *We're leaving for Canada*
and these are the times I hate him
and think he was mean and scared
and wanted to keep us
prisoner in the crude country of his head

ANOTHER LETTER

He gave the address of the bakery where he worked
exactly, down to the postal code, each number carefully drawn
as though she'd be free to visit unannounced
walk through the doors one day and see him, apron tied neatly
around his waist, fingers half buried in white dough

Mai roj kahm kardha, I am working everyday

I wonder if he pictured her, standing in the grey streets of London
the letter in her hands and wind
whipping her *chunni* tight around her throat
wild eyes studying names of streets, brass numbers
nailed above doorways. More likely he knew
she could never find him

HER CREMATION DID NOT FACE THE RISING SUN

One year after
Piari was burned
my father
lay shaking with fever in his straw bed, the heat
rubbing against his skin
like bristling tiger hair. He
spoke strange
vowels. Bugs crawled
over his chest, black and green

Holy men came to the house,
laid their hands on him. Their eyes
rolled back. My grandmother dropped
coins in to their white beards, dirty
tunic bibs
Piari's spirit is fevered, they told her
Her Cremation did not face the rising sun, the ashes
backward in the earth, so now
she cannot rest

In my dreams I have seen her
beyond the wall
where they burned her
pulling at singed hair, wiping
the green stains from her mouth, so scared
She slips in
to my father's chest and hides there
cleans the poison still on her tongue
with his blood

Men from the village exhumed the entire
patch of ground that had mixed
with her remains. Turned it
like a straw mattress and set it down again
seamless in the earth. My grandmother
sat cross-legged in her veils, my father
laid out across her lap
and watched the sun rise

FLOUR (III)

Shivani:

Once, when Piara was sick
there was a drought
and the wheat didn't grow

The fields, miles of straw stocks and yellow dirt
grains swirling in the wind, buffalo crying

He would eat nothing but roti
and there was no wheat

Birds peck. The boy's white bed soaked in sweat
his back a wellspring
open sores blooming in the heat, red yellow black

I pulled my sleeves up;
went into the fields with a bowl

Sun-dust in his throat, stomach crying for bread
his mother's red scarf outside, blowing around her
framed in the window

I plucked single grains
one by one from the ground

Bare feet, back arched, bones knotting
silk sticking, sweat
on her thighs, forehead. Fingers sifting through
dirt, searching

After a long time I filled the bowl
I crushed the wheat and made flour

The boy coughing in the bed, *pani*

Enough for one roti

pounding will and son-love in to the dough

I lit the oven, cooked it

the boy on his back, breathing bread smells
opens his eyes

I looked up and saw the crow
descending

HIS OTHER HEART

In the back of the bakery he read
letters she sent, elbows
propped on the edge of a silver cooling rack
his fingers marking pages
with lard, white flour. A cigarette between his teeth
new habit, one of many, everybody
smokes in London

The rains have come and gone, one letter said
Piara will not open his eyes. And another: *I am tired*
with longing for you. He put the cigarette out
in a plastic ashtray, folded her words
in to his pocket

> *Tdun gadon orna*
> *When will you come?*

Wife, son, daughter. He kept
them in his other heart, the one waiting for him
across the world

THE LEGEND OF GREAT-UNCLE DHARAM

Dharam:

Listen, I'll tell you all I remember—in Delhi
they put me on another train and in Agra
another, the Taj Mahal dirty through the mud-streaked
windows of carriage class. In Lucknow it was the same
cold dahl in a tin bowl, Shivani's roti wrapped up in my sack
I ate and washed with the sway of the train—so many days
that later it felt strange to walk on a steady floor, sit
at a table. Allahabad, Patna, Varanasi, each place
a blur of mud and cloth, rickshaw wheels, brown skin
and in Bodhgaya the flash of cameras, white shirts with collars
sadhus wreathed in their marigolds

One night I walked a road in West Bengal, rested
in a ditch with a family of pigs and fixed my shoe, fell asleep
and woke in the death-sun of afternoon, my tongue stuck
from heat. I rode a bicycle through Dasnager, the rush

of the Ganges close, Calcutta's stink already heavy in the air. Pushed
my feet down hard on the pedals, pictured Piara in his bed
small body stark on the blankets, the deep grooves
around Shivani's mouth. I tell you I pedalled even after
the sun fell, their names like a chanting in my head, tried not to catch
my tires in the holes of the road

It was the only time I ever saw Calcutta, the beggar's city
I moved through the bustee alleys, past fruit carts sticky
with flies, blue nuns and flower-sellers holding out blooms, everywhere
wilted petals underfoot, I came to the temple of Kali
Kalighat
and slit a goat open there
on the tiled floor, from belly to neck
spilt blood across her black feet and fell
to my knees, I remember
my hands shook so badly
for a moment I was afraid

> *Take this instead,* I told her, *Aha Layja*
> *Please take this, and leave*
> *Piara alone*

I never looked at her face once, not even to see
if it changed. Only cleaned my knife and stood, came out
into the light of the street and turned to go back home

TWO STORIES OF MUDFISH

Aaj:

In the pond by the mango grove were mudfish, slick and dark, long as my arm. We spent the afternoons down there trying to catch one, brown clouds of silt under our kicking legs. That was before I could touch the bottom, when Piara would dive down and come back clutching handfuls of pond weed, swearing he had touched a fin, held a tail. I wouldn't put my face in then, not even when Piari threw a thin glass bangle in to the water and told me to get it back; I watched dumbly while it slipped below the surface, shining and green

After, when she died, I went back. Dove in again and again, my fingers searching through the thick muck, fish touching me from all around. I found marbles, orange peels, the bones of a dog. Her bracelet was gone, stuck in the belly of a fish or buried too deep

Piara:

Once when I was sick Aaj brought a fish in the house, one of the ones from the pond with the back fins and long whiskers. I remember him standing in the doorway of the bedroom, brown water dripping from his hair, his shorts. Making a big puddle on the floor. He had it tight in both hands, holding it up like a sword for me to see, his eyes bright and serious. *Ek tdar orna, Piara, I got one*

My mother turned to look and dropped her bowl full of yogurt, screamed so loud that Auntie came running down from the tandoor on the roof. I remember the two of them squealing, feet stamping around like in a dance, jewelry flashing, their hands wild. And Aaj's laugh, the sound of it rushing through the house like cool water soothing my fever

LETTER TO AN AILING SON

(Never mailed)

Sundar:

Outside my window
a cold England moon. This letter
is to tell you it is not the same
Not the same moon
you sweat and shiver under, my son

See, when I come back
I will take you to Bikaner
for the festival of the Desert City
where men eat and breath fire
in the dark
they spit and stamp in deep pits of ash, open
mouths like burning hoops
through which the soul jumps

Stand still enough
outside the fire-breathers' circle
and it is like you are watching the start of the world
Every spark cast off the tongue makes
a fresh wound in the blackness
a hole for each of us to slip through
and be born
First you, my son, then me
we will come out clean on the other side
clean beneath an Indian moon

When I come back
When I come back

*

Back

ॐ

Sundar:

Imagine you are caught. A snare
made from rope or chain
or flesh. Long ago when I was ten there were gypsies
who came through Pubwan selling metal toys, their clothes
made of torn cloth—all colours
like the dancers of Rajasthan. One was my age
and said he could read anyone's future
by looking deep
into the nail of their thumb. *Give me your hands,* he said
and I did. We were only boys but his fingers
were sharp and dry and his cheek
had a scar that was round, swollen like a seed
I learned to see my hands then
He showed me the way they curved just so
ready for the handle of a plow, a knife
a woman's breast. *I see two sons and more*
daughters, he said to me
and that day I made my hands into two fists
hard and tight and able to hold
nothing

After that my nights were filled
with quick bursts of dream—
a splash of blood on bristled fur
a spread wing pinned

DOLLS

Shivani:

When I was a girl
I made dolls. Collected
fabric scraps from under my mother's
bench, snagged the bright bits
from her old saris before
she used them as rags. Once
I found a piece of machete blade in the wheat field
and tried to cut up my auntie's best red *chunni*
the one that was the color of Bombay lips. My hands
were too small to use a dull blade on silk
I dropped the tatters into the well so she
would never know, watched them fall into the darkness
like red kisses

In the shade of houses the village girls sat
in half-circles, away from the boys. Working our bent needles
our coarse black thread. We stitched doll faces, mouths
upturned lines of closed smiles. Wove yarn
into *surma* around the eyes. Dancing dresses
in purples and golds, skirts
that twirled up around cotton legs. Once
a boy came running into us, chasing
a wheel rim, his bare chest
heaving. He stumbled and
grasped my shoulder, laughing. Broke
our circle

That was the year that my grandmother
kept me from school, her eyes on me
in the kitchen while I pounded dough. *Not*
enough hard, she told me, *your fingers*
too weak. She whispered about men, her voice
like a dull blade through silk. Gave me
a pot of *surma,* black as thread. I watched
friends pass my window on their way to school
new dolls in their hands
I pulled up water from the well for tea, waited
to pull up kisses

MATCHMAKER

Shivani:

In a field between Pubwan
and Matudah there is a tree
black with bats. Ten thousand wings
beat there, shiver like leaves
around the warm fruit of ten thousand bodies.
It is said
that to sleep on the roots of this tree
will bring an answer to any question in the form
of a dream. At fourteen, three nights
before my wedding
I told no one, packed a bag
with bread and a blanket, slipped away
from my mother's house
as Ratha Siwami read the evening blessing

At the village gates I stopped, stared
into the dark ahead and breathed. I pictured
the tree in its field, branches
heavy with ten thousand shining eyes, each one
a window to look through
and see my fate: the face
of a boy in Pubwan awake in his bed, soon
to be married, he is fourteen too. I knew
in three nights I would leave the village
and never return to my mother's house. That night
I did not step outside the gates

Sundar:

Three nights before I married
there was a party in my father's house
and candles burned in rows
on the rooftop. It was in this light
that I met the *Betcholi,* matchmaker, old woman
with a mouth that drooped on one side
Nikka Purrahnah, she said and pinched
my cheek, *I will send you a dream tonight*
of your bride
After she turned her back, my brother
hooked a finger in his lip and pulled, stuck out his tongue
You'll dream
of the village goat, he said to me, and grinned

But I did not sleep. After the candles went out I lay
in bed and felt the air
press down on me, took the sounds
of my father's house in to my body:
stripped hides twisting on their lines, a paw
scratching at stone, Dharam's steady breath.
I saw nothing. Kept
my hands fisted in the dark, heartbeat
contained in each tight palm. When I closed my eyes
it was the rush of my own blood I heard
the noise of it
like the shivering of leaves in a sudden wind
ten thousand wings, startled into flight

HER PLACE

Shivani:

The Taj Mahal has rooms below it
set with jewels. I was there once
long ago, reached out
to touch a ruby in the wall
pressed my hand over it and wished

After six months of waiting for him she took work
in a cafeteria downtown serving
lunch lines, wore a stiff apron and white shoes, absorbed
shallow language. *Lemon pie, clam chowder*
coffee decaf. Learned to point at the specials board
if her accent was too thick, fill styrofoam bowls
without letting the ladle drip. There are ways
to do the impossible—she learned her place
all over again

On Blackhall street the immigrant wives
watched her come home at six, stared
though the gaps in their kitchen drapes while they stirred
spinach saag, saffron rice
chickpeas on the stove. *Aiya, Can you believe it?* they said
Her husband has still not come. Her father
wrote more letters to England, each one sharper
than the last, more full of words for shame. Nights
she wrapped her head with fine bright silk, wore jeweled slippers
that sparkled in the TV light

FLOUR (IV)

Early before school my father walked
the empty Victoria streets and didn't dream
of bicycles. Oblivious
to pitching-arm warm-ups he hiked
the driveways, placed a paper gently
on each doorstep. Sixty-two
every weekday and eighty-six on Sundays
all worth a penny apiece. He counted
the cents as he stooped
to lay each paper on a welcome mat
(Ten for a comic book, five
for a bag of licorice)
One hundred and fifty
for a sack of flour

CAGE

Aaj:

Words reach out of the air, English
and Punjabi rearrange themselves
breed together
ugly burst of sound, vowels
falling out like groans; glue them
back in   remade words
letters hanging off my fingers by their hooks
and holes

Here is a bird: *chirdii.*
c-beaked, winged, i's are bars
of its cage

Piara teaches Mahnji Lali "mother",
"father". Sister
              Auntie
              Uncle
His accent gets leaner; turn sideways and it
disappears. I hold out letters to him
feathers plucked
from exotic wings. Wait for me, *paraji*
Wait for me, brother

ॐ

Piara:

This is the position for a beating at school: squat right down
elbows tucked in, hold on
to your ears. Now curl your toes
in the dirt and use them—shift yourself backward
the moment the strap comes down, anticipate, lean in
to the blow, the leather will be worn
in the middle, far kinder than the wicked tip
This is the trick that every brown boy knows

> He was eight when men from Unicef came to the village, bags of powdered milk slung over their shoulders. He watched them from the window of the one-room school while they worked, neatly stacking supplies, short hair hidden under blue cloth caps. Two years later, in the basement on Blackhall Street he would remember it, the way they moved like unfamiliar animals, the landscape around them alternately holding its breath and remaking itself as they entered and exited

But North Ward Elementary is different
you must stand still, hold out
your hand, palm up. There is no means to soften it
your toes are cased in shoes, the dirt
in concrete. The strap comes down
where it wants
and when it wants: for not knowing
that a bell means the end of lunch, looking
out the window, for speaking Punjabi
in class

In a Victoria schoolyard he stands with his brother amidst bars and swings, metal slides. He is waiting for Uncle Dharam to bring them food, warm dahl and bread in a covered bowl. His hands hang quiet, palms raw from the strap. Later the skin will heal, and be broken, and heal again, until he learns the trick that all white boys know. But for now he is a new animal crafted from both fur and feathers, nostrils lined with strange spices, eyes a nameless colour. Around him, the schoolyard shudders, and exhales and remakes itself

THE MATTER BETWEEN ANIMAL AND MACHINE IS

Once a hunter killed a goat and watched
the guts come out, saw the concrete cracks
on the floor of his garage grab at the gore
Puddles move, blood running
like children racing out
to the road. Alarmed
the police arrived to intervene
You can't   kill a goat, not at home

In India, my father never saw
a plane till he was ten. Imagine
if at birth your eyes were bound with black tape
and then at ten you tore it off and saw:
the enormous lightning beast leaping
through distance, white animal growing
with each blink. "Have you ever heard
a tiger as it kills?" says my father
"It is exactly the sound that a plane
makes when it lands." *We crept in to its belly*
felt the rumblings as it digested us

Piara:

> After only a week of Canada
> your grandfather bought a goat
> and slaughtered it in the garage while neighbors
> mowed their lawns

The belly
of the great white tiger hanging over him
skyless

I TRIED TO FIND INDIA IN ITS POETS

I wanted to see a picture of the Punjab
in words, to smell the wood doorsteps
covered with hay
and wild yellow chrysanthemums, the very same
my grandmother threw her wash water on
when she was just a young woman
Souza
Jussawalla
Ramanujan
I tried to find a picture in words

Old stories—Siddhartha, Vishnu, Black Kali
all dusty statues, huge toes and frozen hair
sandalwood arms
And new stories—grocery chain stores, airports, catbells and cars
none in between
none that inhabit the space it takes
a yellow flower to grow up around a wood doorstep

I tried to find India in its poets
but I couldn't
they are too busy
finding themselves

I wanted to see a mango tree
in the center of a field, men
melting sugar beneath it, to smell
the cane bake, iron pot flake
the wooden paddles stirring. I looked
for a word that would tell me
the color of shade
the size of a mango tree leaf, and the length
of its shadow at noon. A word
that would show me the black faces of monkeys
paws outstretched gripping a red fruit. What
do I want with airports, catbells and cars?

I tried to find India in its poets
but they are too busy finding Canada
in me

I've never seen her
my grandmother
chrysanthemums the color of lemon rind
around the hem of her dress
tossing the wash water
out of the door
I looked for a poet to tell me
how she looked then
when her cheeks were smooth like warm sugar syrup
lips red as mangos
how did she look

FEARING INDIA

Everyone says
the begging is the worst. So many hands
palms up, ready to catch
coins, food, the extra fat
on your chin. *Be reasonable about it*
they tell me. *Don't give to everyone*
or you'll never get home

Tonight I am unable to sleep
my bags packed, round-trip ticket
on my dresser. I fear India, the brown hands
paler palms, empty. They surround
the bed, fingers so close but never
touching. I count bones in the room,
the new moon in my window a white rib

    In the dark I seal my mouth and
    trap appetite. Learn
    to re-ingest myself, calorie by calorie
    Beg my insides to turn out
    and into empty palms

When I am thin as grass
I will walk upright
in my father's village
sprinkle money like seeds
in the fields until it is gone
all gone
and I can never get home

FLIGHT OVER CALCUTTA

The old woman two seats over
calls our blond stewardess a *Surmuni*
The first
of many translations my father
will have to make, I'm sure. I get up
and walk the aisle, stand outside the washroom, balanced
over Calcutta, each foot
on a border

Surmuni: One who chops off her hair.
Huh?

Another question. Almost there.

ॐ

The Punjab, Pubwan, the Jalandhar District
population one thousand
three days journey to Delhi in the heat
wheat and watermelon, corn
kinnows, cane and squash

Back

FROM MY NOTEBOOK:

November 30th, 2001, in a jeep on the way to Pubwan, 2:12 am

We deplane and drive through Delhi in the dark, past a confusion of all-night fruit stands, figures bundled in filthy cloth, fires burning in the street. Fluorescent tubes wired to trees along the road streak by like gunshots, illuminate signs that sell shampoo, pickled mango, Aristocrat Whiskey. Cows everywhere. They paw at the garbage, the gravel hills of construction sites. At a roadside midway we stop to use the bathroom, my father waits outside while I learn to maneuver a Punjabi toilet, just a hole in the floor. He calls instructions from outside the door, *Squat down, keep the weight on your legs.* I am tired, embarrassed, numb. All certainty vanishes.

ॐ

Dogs run in packs
through the streets of Matudah, Pubwan, Bhanapur
steal chapattis from temple offerings, scratch
each other, piss on lampposts
Tonight a group of them have come
to howl outside my father's room, a song
for their ancestral savior

FIRST LESSON

Each morning at breakfast I watch her
from the balcony, my hands tight
around a warm glass of *chai*. She has been there
three days now on the wellhouse roof, crouched
down, her white scarf loose around her
long grey hair. *Sick*, is all my buppa tells me
when I ask about her. *Not long now*
I sip tea while she coughs deep
spits again in the gravel

Below in the square the village boys
are playing *baat*, knocking marbles together in the heat
and from the temple kitchen sounds of women making rotis
hands clapping around balls of soft dough. Somewhere
the shoeshiner calls out from his cart, *pange rupieay*
I want to ask them if they know
a woman is up on the wellhouse roof, waiting
to die

But they know. I sip my tea while she spits, take the sounds
of this village into my body as she has done
day after day, the howl of dogs, noise of peacocks, morning
prayers from the temple doorway. Today
my family and I will go to Nurmahal and shop for silk,
eat fruit from a roadstand and not stop
to think of her. What else can be said? Things are
as they are

ALL THAT'S LEFT

Piari, I stand on all that's left
of your grave, walk in your overgrown places
ask neighbors, the woman who sweeps the house
to remember, write down what they say
in my notebook, still not enough of you
to fill one page

> *She liked to read, wore her hair loose*
> *even though it was not the style, fed*
> *seeds to the parrots and saarks*
> *green bangles that clinked*
> *when her hand was raised in school*
> *She was the best at making corn pop*
> *on an open fire*

FOR MY NOTEBOOK

Chaginder, the childhood
rival of my father, now
a sari salesman
Calling out to ladies
who pass his little shop, the word "sister", *behenji*
comes off his lips with ease

> *Lenga, suit*
> *salwar kamiz, sister*

He smiles from a pink lawnchair
in the doorway. Beer belly
gold rope around his neck—
exactly as I've pictured. Fat
kauva, yes, unmistakable
I eat bananas with him, take care
where I cast my shadow. Tell me, *brother*
what do you have for my notebook?

> *She got the strap a lot*
> *for laughing during lessons. And once*
> *on the way to temple*
> *I used my guli dunda stick to lift up the back*
> *of her dress*

ॐ

built in the shade of invisible trees
cold corner of herdland, I stand
in the stone house where my grandfather learned
to walk and bare his teeth

these windowless rooms I have seen before
only in dreams
where I fall

SECOND LESSON

Buppa, you can't
escape me now. I've seen the house
where you were born   son
of tanners, seen
the hides that twist on lines
watched your cousins scrape the stretched skins clean
with knives. Don't turn away. I've seen the room
where you were born, know what you saw
when you opened your tiny eyes:
four thick walls of mud and hair, the leather
coat and mask you'd wear   forever
disguised. I've seen
what's underneath, don't turn away. Come with me
to the place where you were born
see the hands that touched you, hang hides
on the lines to dry   son
of tanners, I know where the paddle and whip
fit, which hook is for which
inside you
blood   my blood too

FOR MY UNCLE

Here is the earthen house
where you grew, six walls that hold
every shadow of your remembrance. Light
falls through these windows at the same soft angles, the old beds
are in the same place. On this patch of floor
a two-headed snake showed itself once
and vanished through a hole, your mouth
wide in surprise. And there
is the corner where they bandaged your eyes with tape
and told you it was just a trick of shade. But, no. You can't

come back here yet, go forward. Fourteen years old
watching TV on Blackhall and your father
arrives from England, the apparition of his face
finally made flesh. His jaw is set, he wears
a hat and suit. Kneel to touch
his feet as you were taught, the raindrops
on the cuffs of his pants wipe off on your cheeks, roll
down again like tears. Who is this man? Standing
in the living room with two grown boys
crouched at his shoes. He puts his suitcase down, crushes
the ghost that has walked with you in both halves
of the world. Later this man
will pour a drink and sit at the kitchen table
peel an apple with a knife and put his hands
on your mother. Go forward

again and step in front of the thrown
fist meant for your brother. You take
the punch for him and stagger, head smacking
the wall

Sundar's boy—you have learned to say *Father*
in two tongues, speak neither with the slightest trace
of an accent. There are some words that stick
inside the skin and gleam like bars
of a cage. I know
I am forbidden to write such words, *these* words
on a page, even if it is burned and the ashes
burned again. But this poem is to say:

I believe you. Two-headed snakes, though rare
are found in the secret places of this world, under the edges
of buildings and rocks, beneath the sand, inside mud walls. Only
a few have ever
seen them in the light. Burn this page
if you must, but come back to this earthen house and see
it is the same as you remember. I will wait here for you
as a witness

ANOTHER STORY: NUR MAHAL

Piara:

But listen, I've never told you
about the rains, have I?
Caught outside in monsoon
the world turns to water
in three breaths:
the first, a gasp of shock, and
then, the slow exhale
of understanding. Third
is a challenge to the sky: the lungs take in
their limit and the body
gets ready
to run

Rain engulfs the land
before dirt can melt to mud, drowns plants
before they drink. In villages
the sudden water
blinds oxen, dissolves
even the surest step. But in the towns
there's real danger, live wires fall
from poles and rooftops. Sizzle
in the water and make it poison, milk-white
stinging barbs, I've seen just
one shallow inch
kill a man

Here, under the great serai arch of Nur Mahal
my father and grandmother once
hid from a storm. Caught out
in the streets she used a scarf and
two breaths
to shield his passport photo from the rains (a last chance
on paper, her son finally awake
and strong, she must
keep it dry) And one more breath
to grab his wrist and run

Together, under this arch
they waited while just outside the wires
fell like arrows, poison-tipped with certain aim
white-water barbs that grabbed
the ankles of a man and shook him
made each muscle shudder in a frenzied dance
before he fell
just inches from their feet

I put my hand to sandstone
dry and warm. This serai
has sheltered strays and soldiers
stood near enough for most
to reach in three breaths. Once
it saved a woman, her son
and a last chance. I came here
to finish the story: touch this wall and leave
my invisible print

THIRD LESSON

Here
is the unnamed
tree you could not show me
with your words, at last
made real. See the frail
alphabet as it falls away
all the suffering vowels, desirous
phrase, the ash
of image

Stop your tongue and I
will stop my pen; no speech
can stop
or start
the pulse of this tree, no ink
can change it. Here
is one branch
strong enough to hold
your weight and mine. Sit with me
in silence

FEAT

Seven a.m. and Mahnji ties
a black cotton kerchief around my head
sends me out
in to the cool stone square
with a basket. *Baarr unday,* she says
again, leans in
so I can see the way her lips
make words. *Baar-r. Un-day.*

She watches
as I cross the square to the village shop
open my mouth
deep intake of
breath. *Baarr unday,* I say. *Twelve*
eggs.

I return with my basket
full of what will be
our breakfast. Twelve eggs
exactly, no more
no less. I hold them up to her
the fruits
of my great feat.

FOURTH LESSON

Indian history isn't
Piara
Dharam
Shivani
Tage

but a lineage of one
title: Chaudri, Kumari, Singh
the study of a common birthmark
a chronicle of unmixed blood

(So I break the line, my Mahnji?
Aachaa. You break
the line.)

GOOD BEGGARS

I move through Akbar's jasper fort
past boys and girls balanced
in marble doorways, skinny backs
against the carved reliefs of kings
their bare toes curled on stone posts
that once chained elephants
        ma'am-sir fifty rupee
books of postcards, glossy blues and greens

> (A lame child leans on crutches, offers clay beads, I pass
> her by. *Their parents are to blame,* the guides have told
> us. *You mustn't*
> *encourage it. Bound legs make for good beggars*)

Choices haunt me. Six hundred
concubines have climbed the emperor's steps
Courtesans and queens have sipped
from silver here. I carry a camera, my shoes
are new. How
can I pass her by? But I do, I do.

THE ROAD TO JAIPUR

On the road to Jaipur there are men who keep bears
spear metal hooks
through each animal nostril. My father and I drive by these in a taxi
and the men make their bears do tricks for us, up on back legs
paws raking at the bright Indian sun. I close my eyes
and I am the bear, mind drowning in chain-noise, collar
choked around my neck. Or I am the man with the whip
and the hard mouth, flies
crawling inside my collar, fists closed
I open my eyes and know
I am neither one. My father is seated beside me, hands
quiet in his lap, face hushed as scenes
go by outside: a man, a bear, dust, pavement. No metaphors
to be found

PRAYER FOR MY FATHER

To Kali, India, 2001

Dharam:

Shivani, wife
of my only brother
what you do not know of my heart would fill these
bowls
one hundred times. Heavy as one hundred coins were Kali's eyes,
and brighter too
I never looked at Her face once
that is what I told you. But oh, She looked at mine
and knew my heart
and still knows. In Calcutta is a secret you will never find
But take these bowls from my hands
and wash the blood away. Light candles. Make
offerings. Your son
is safe and She is appeased

Black Kali
goddess of the lost
goddess of the sick
I invoke you
the steady girth of Ganesh behind me, his chariot rats
restless in their ropes, swift claws ready
to carry me away should I cry out in fear
But my jaw is set, I hold
one tusk in each fist
and call

Kalighat
I will sit crosslegged in your house until you come
four brass bowls upturned at my feet
            See them, they are the same four
that caught blood from the goat offered to you
the same four
Dharam carried home on his weary back. For long years
they have been bathed in sugared milk and splashed
with candle wax, held more grain in winter
than would fill a belly

I have found a cold and quiet
room in your house
to make this prayer. I have no meat to fill these
bowls
that would be sweet enough
for such a taste as yours. My own brown flesh
is pale, poison to you, it catches
in the teeth. My blood is thin as water
in this country. But I am still my father's child

and he is tethered to your arms
an old black thread that stretches
over fields and seas and in
to his ailing bones. *Tuberculosis*
Heart Disease
Pancreatitis
He has survived all three in both worlds and still
has strength enough to hide me
from your eyes. But now, here, I hold my wrists to you, jaw set
in challenge and wait
for a thread to be tied

Take this instead and leave
my father alone

But you will not come. My wrists are bare
and free. I uncross my legs, lay down
the tusks. Send rats to the shadows
where they vanish among other ghosts. There
is my great uncle, scruff of the goat
in his hand, knife poised. And there is my father as a boy
shaking the shroud of sickness from his shoulders
and shaking me to my feet

Black Kali
goddess of the lost
goddess of the sick
Though I beg for it
you cannot know my heart. My father guards against it
even in the rooms of your house. His blood
is vigilant, and thick, and flows enough to
fill one hundred bowls of brass
and more. *Lick them clean Kali,* he says. *Be appeased.*

LIST (THE LAST LESSONS)

From my notebook, India, 2001

Save candles and a match
to light the streets, never
depend on electric
the web of wire above has been here since
the British came, will fail for certain
on a dark walk home

A woman alone on the dark streets of Delhi:
fair game. Men standing
in hollow doorways like the looks
of half-brown skin, so have
an escort. Shirt buttons: the topmost
two are fine left open, but the third—
do up tight. A scarf to mask
exhaust in gridlock also
covers the head and face
from temple to temple. And ankles? Don't be
a prude, India
is a modern country. Leave beige
behind. Colour
was created for a reason
so was stitchery, the *khadi* looms, though steady
still spin with abandon

Save small bills
save large coins
for beggars, enough
but not too much. And don't touch
strays, they carry the red foam
and fever. Village butchers
will cut meat with *gaarca* knives
held in their toes. And those who
tan the hides know the trick
of self-reliance: what the skin
can stand before it breaks. Save
all judgement
for another time
and place

A fact: only girls born
and raised in India
are good at making *rotis* round. Another:
crouching is an art
that's in the bones. Indians
can do without chairs if need be, but please
tea is taken at a table
From my mahnji: *Never take tea*
offered by a stranger in a doorway
Carry your own water
carry your own cup

Save some secrets. Not everything
will flourish in open light. A torn
photograph, masala recipe, healed
bruise. An old man's guilt. The location
of a tree in high woods. Above all remember
to sing, to dance. Wear skirts boldly
with decoration, catch the sun on hem
and wrist. Be brave
be a daughter
of the field and soil and stone
Carry your own cup
Spin with abandon

PIARI APPEARS IN A DREAM

India, 2001

Remember, I was only seven
limbs half-grown, hair in braids. I never
knew wisdom, I lived and died, I can't
love you. Hush. You will belong
to India with
or without me

ॐ

In my India there is still
a secret garden
where the *bulbul* sings my father's name. But listen close
there is a song with my name, also. I have walked
with tigers, lived
in palaces of gold. I will whisper
the tale to you. Tell no one

GLOSSARY OF TERMS

baat – children's game played with marbles
bahenji – sister
barr – twelve
betcholi – matchmaker
beti – daughter
bhangra – a dancing party; also a form of music
bulbul – Indian nightingale
chai – tea sweetened with sugar and milk, often spiced
chirdii – bird
chunni – traditional women's scarf
dahl – simple curry made from lentils and spices
dukh – ultimate pain, sorrow
Ganesh – Indian god with the head of an elephant. Often depicted with one broken tusk, which He broke in order to use as a writing instrument
gaarca – type of butcher's knife held by the feet
guli dunda – a children's game played with stones and sticks
gurdwara – temple
jalebi – a sugary Indian sweet
Kali / Black Kali – Indian goddess of chaos and destruction
kameez – tunic shirt worn by women
kauva – crow
laddu – an Indian sweet made with flour and sugar, usually in the shape of a ball
lenga – women's outfit consisting of tunic or top and long skirt
naht – run
pakora – battered and fried vegetables or meat mixed with spices
pani – water
paraji – brother
roti – flatbread

rupee – Indian currency
saag – curry made with spinach
salwar kamiz – women's outfit consisting of loose trousers and tunic
surma – traditional liquid black eyeliner
shaa – shadow
supp – snake or serpent
unday – eggs

ACKNOWLEDGEMENTS

I would like to thank everyone who contributed to the shaping and editing of this book, including Hiro Boga, Patricia Young, BJ Christensen, Carol Myhre, and most especially, Marilyn Bowering. I would also like to thank my family, my friend, Damen Djos, and my partner, Oakley Thompson, for their patience and unwavering support.

Danielle Lagah was born in 1977 in Victoria, British Columbia, to parents of mixed cultural background. Her mother is of Scottish descent, and her father, an immigrant from the farmlands of Northern India, infused her childhood with stories of his Punjabi heritage and experiences. Much of Danielle's writing incorporates this infusion; her poetry, in particular, focuses on the immigrant experience of merging cultures. Her work has appeared in literary journals and anthologies, on CBC radio and in short-form film.

Danielle travels to India and China several times a year for her work as a wholesale home décor buyer and stylist, a profession that allows her to constantly observe the effects and nuances of cross-culturalization. She lives in Nanoose Bay with her partner, Oakley, and their Scottish Fold cat, Zampano.

RECENT OOLICHAN TITLES

Leaving the Farm • Ross Klatte
". . . both a haunting elegy for a way of life that is fast disappearing and a beautifully crafted memoir about the universal experience of growing up. *Leaving the Farm* is life-writing at its best."
—Ken McGoogan

Notes for a Rescue Narrative • J. Mark Smith
"With this collection J. Mark Smith reveals himself as one of the most imaginative and accomplished young poets in Canada."
—Eric Ormsby

The Blue Sky • Galsan Tschinag
"With this novel, a Mongolian shaman has stepped onto the stage of world literature."—*Der Spiegel*

Words • Mark Ellis
Illustrated by Ruth Campbell
"A stunning combination of word and image . . ."

Silent Inlet • Joanna Streetly
"A great book to curl up in a corner with . . . I loved it."
—Phyllis Reeve

To view our complete catalogue, visit us online at
www.oolichan.com